THE FALL
OF THE
RED STAR

"An excellent story—it is exciting and personal, and conveys a deep sense of the great gift of freedom."
—*School Library Journal*

"Powerful writing, a riveting eyewitness account . . . I highly recommend *The Fall of the Red Star* to readers of all ages, but especially to the young who would like to read about brave young heroes."
—Gabor Bodnar
Secretary General, Hungarian Scout Association of America

"A solid addition to collections of historical fiction."
—*Voice of Youth Advocates*

"A 'must read' for anyone who cares about hope, courage, and love of freedom."
—Edith K. Lauer, Hungarian American Coalition

"An extraordinary book. I am also a survivor of those turbulent years in Hungary. I can testify as an eyewitness to the shocking authenticity of the story. It is one of the most effective indictments of Communism to appear in a book for young adults."
—Clara Gyorgyey
President, International P.E.N. Club

- NCSS-CBC Notable Social Studies Trade Books for Young People
- A Bank Street College Book of the Year
- Washington Press Association Communicator of Excellence Award
- National Federation of Press Women Juvenile Book Fiction Award

THE FALL
OF THE
RED STAR

Helen M. Szablya
Peggy King Anderson

Boyds Mills Press

For my husband, Dr. John F. Szablya and our seven children, three of whom escaped with us, and all of whom are freedom-fighters, as well as to their spouses, and our thirteen grandchildren, and those not born yet.

H.M.Sz.

For my daddy, Frank King, on his way to the best Freedom of all.

P.K.A.

And for all who gave their lives for freedom.

Text copyright © 1996 by Helen M. Szablya and Peggy King Anderson

Published by Boyds Mills Press, Inc.
A Highlights Company
815 Church Street
Honesdale, Pennsylvania 18431
Printed in the United States of America

Publisher Cataloging-in-Publication Data
Szablya, Helen, M.
    Fall of the red star / by Helen M. Szablya and Peggy King Anderson. —1st ed.
[128]p. : ill. ; cm.
Summary : Fourteen-year-old Stephen takes up arms and joins the resistance in this novel of the Hungarian Revolution.
ISBN: 1-56397-977-2
I. Hungary — History — Revolution, 1956 — Juvenile fiction. [1. Hungary — History — Revolution — , 1956 — Fiction.] 1. Anderson, Peggy King. II. Title.
813.54 — dc20   [F]   1996   AC
Library of Congress Catalog Card Number 95-76351

First Boyds Mills Press paperback edition, 2001
Book designed by Jamie Levanowitz.
The text of the book is set in 12-point Berkeley Book.
Cover illustration by Peter Catalanotto

10 9 8 7 6 5 4 3 2 1

The authors would like to acknowledge the following experts for helping make this book possible: Our editor, Megan McDonald, who saw the potential and drew it out; Dr. John F. Szablya, Helen's husband, for his geographical and historical knowledge of Budapest and Hungary; Dr. Zoltán Kramár, military historian; and Mrs. Mária Kramár, freedom fighter, both ardent Hungarian scouts who read through the manuscript for accuracy.

We would like to thank all those scout leaders who continued scouting illegally in Hungary after it had been outlawed in April 1948. Some of these leaders spent years in prison for their courage. We thank all those who lived the Revolution and those who died for freedom. We thank Marcey Painter Szablya for her assistance in the rewrite and for doing the glossary. Special thanks to Michael K. Anderson for his help and guidance in writing Stephen's *Freedom* Overture, the mythical journey of the White Stag.

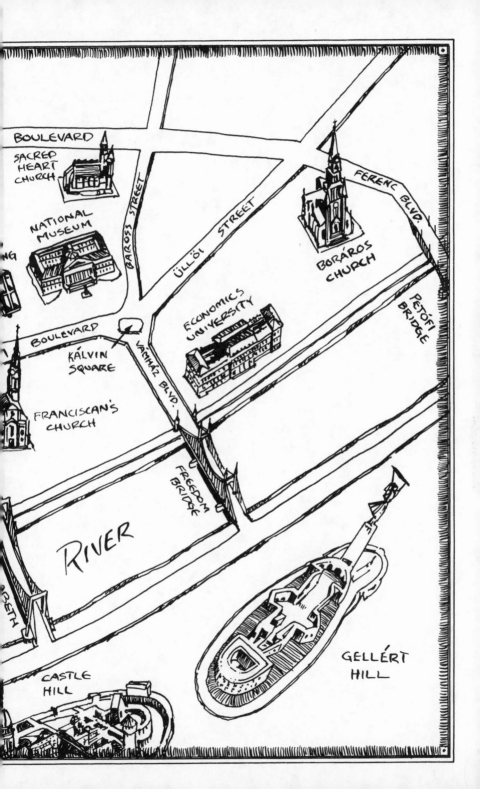

Prologue

"The White Stag leapt across the blue-flowing river. They followed him, those two heroic sons of Enéh. Then Magyar and Hunor entered that beautiful land where the grass is silk and the water sweet, and honey drips from the tree-hollows . . . Their new homeland."

(From the ancient Hungarian legend of the White Stag)

Budapest, Hungary
October 21, 1948

Footsteps thudded on the stairs outside their apartment. Six-year-old Stephen turned in his sleep, hoping to go back into his dream, the dream of the White Stag.

It had been a good day in the country. He and his big sister, Mária, laughed and ran after the chickens squawking in the grassy yard. They dangled a ribbon in front of Miska, the half-grown cat, and tumbled with her in the fallen leaves.

And Apu told him the story of the White Stag who led Magyar and his brother into Hungary long, long ago.

Stephen loved the stories Apu told him about the White Stag. Still, he'd been tired on the long train ride home. He'd fallen asleep in the warmth of his father's arms, and missed the end of the story.

Now it was late at night and he was back in his bed here in the city, and the footsteps coming up the stairs were louder.

BANG. BANG. BANG.

Stephen sat up in bed, his heart thumping. Who could be at their door in the middle of the night? He heard the murmur of voices from his parents' bedroom, and a rustling sound as his father pulled on his clothes.

Stephen leaned forward to stare into the murky shadows of the parlor. He could just see the silhouette of Anyu, his mother, with Apu right behind her.

Then the click of the switch, and yellow light knifed into the bedroom. Stephen winced and covered his eyes for a moment.

BANG. BANG. BANG. The pounding at the door again. He saw the look his mother gave Apu, and his heart clutched tight in his chest. Why did they not hurry to answer the door? Something was terribly wrong.

Mária was still asleep in her bed beside his. She could sleep through anything.

BANG. BANG. BANG.

Stephen watched, waited.

His father unbolted the door.

Two men in uniform, their boots gleaming in the harsh yellow light.

"István Kôváry?"

Apu nodded.

"You will come with us."

Apu's shoulders slumped. Stephen saw the whiteness of his mother's face. She looked so slight, even in her heavy robe.

"What is the charge?" his father asked.

"You know very well!" The AVO officer's voice was loud, painful to Stephen's ears.

"Please," Anyu said. "The children. They are asleep."

Mária awoke suddenly and sat up. Creeping to Stephen's bed, she reached out and took his small hand in her own. Her hand was icy cold.

Anyu hurried now, putting clothes into a bag. She was almost out of Stephen's line of vision, but he saw her hands fumble as she shoved Apu's heavy sweater, a knit cap, and a pair of woolen socks into the small duffel bag.

"We have no time for this!" the officer shouted.

"At least his coat. It is so cold."

"Come with us now!" The AVO man grabbed his father's shoulder, and Apu fell, his head hitting the small wooden table by the door.

Stephen jumped up, but Mária pulled him back, putting a warning hand over his mouth.

A rivulet of blood trickled down Apu's forehead as he struggled to get to his feet. Stephen stared, fascinated by the shiny red line moving down his father's cheek.

Anyu stood beside Apu, her hand pressed against her mouth, the knuckles white. Apu stood up. "You do not need to do this. I will go with you." He turned to Anyu. "Good-bye, Margit. Kiss the children for me."

His father's voice was calm, determined, but it did not sound like his own. He kissed Anyu then, holding her face for a moment between his hands. The AVO officers standing in the hall shouted out another command.

His father was gone.

Mária gave a little gasp, and released Stephen's hand. He looked down and saw the red welt on his wrist, where she had squeezed it so tightly.

He jumped off the bed and ran to the bedroom window, peering outside to the narrow street. Three shadows moved quickly down the front steps of the apartment and into the bright light of the street lamp. The two AVO officers, Apu between them.

The taller one jerked open the door of a black car parked at the curb, and climbed in. The other officer pushed Apu into the car and slid in after him. The door slammed, and the car sped away.

Mária pressed her fists against her mouth and began to cry with sharp little noises, like Miska when her tail got caught in the door.

Apu had not cried, not even when he fell. Stephen would not cry either, though his sister looked blurred now as he stood stiffly beside her.

He did not know what else to do. He reached his arms around Mária and held on tight, tight.

Chapter 1
The Unexpected Visitor

EIGHT YEARS LATER

St. Endre Island, Budapest, Hungary,
October 20, 1956

Stephen stretched his cramped legs and peered out from behind the hazelnut bush. The setting sun glinted off the Danube River, just visible between the trees.

Pali was nowhere in sight. Stephen frowned. "Do you see him?"

Dini shook his head. "He's way over on the other side of that blackberry patch. He won't look here for a good ten minutes. Besides, it's just a game, Stephen." He felt in his pockets. "I'm hungry. Do you have anything with you?"

"You're always hungry. Here. I saved half a sandwich from lunch." Stephen pulled the crushed bread and lard from his pocket and handed it to Dini. "You know, if there *is* fighting, this won't be just a game anymore."

"There won't be fighting." Dini brushed his curly dark hair back with one hand. "Little Hungary taking on Soviet tanks? It won't happen."

"Pali's convinced it *will* happen."

Dini rolled his eyes and took another bite of sandwich.

From the distance came a low vibrating sound. Stephen stiffened. "Did you hear that? Sounded like a boat motor."

"Relax, Stephen." Dini settled down comfortably behind an alder tree. "George will keep a good lookout. Besides, the AVO can't be bothered patrolling every little cove around here."

"I hope you're right." Stephen sat down beside Dini. A bird trilled in the branches above him. The bird trilled again, a curious three notes, each one higher than the one before. Stephen listened, holding the notes in his mind.

Perfect. These would be the opening notes for his new piano piece. His fingers itched, eager to play the melody that unfolded in his thoughts.

A twig cracked loudly on the other side of the clearing. He stood up. "Wait here, Dini. This time, I'll get Pali." Stephen crept down the hill, weaving his way between the tangled bushes. All he had to do was spot Pali and call out the numbers on his cap. Then Pali would be "dead," and for once *he,* Stephen, would win this game!

No sound of Pali now, but he was probably close by. Stephen edged his way toward the blackberry patch.

A rustling of leaves behind him. He turned, startled.

"Two-five-zero-nine!" Pali yelled triumphantly.

Stephen took off his cap, looked at the numbers, then threw it down on the ground. "How did you get here so quickly? I was watching for you."

"I circled around while you daydreamed. Still writing music in your head?" Pali grinned, then looked past Stephen toward the little stand of alder trees. "Could that be Dini up there?"

Stephen, following his gaze, caught a glimpse of Dini's blue jacket poking out from behind the tree. He still rested comfortably, probably eating his sandwich. Stephen sighed.

Pali headed up the hill toward the thicket. Stephen slumped down on a moss-covered log.

He could never win against Pali. Ever since he'd begun school they'd played together, and Pali always won. Stephen remembered his sister, Mária, consoling him. "It's all right, Stephen. You are good at other things."

"What?" Stephen had asked.

"Playing the piano, for one," she'd said.

That was true. His grandmother had given him lessons on the old Bösendorfer from the time he was four. He remembered trying to get his pudgy fingers to stretch from key to key as he played his first songs. His mother and father had watched so proudly.

His father. Apu.

That long ago memory seemed like a dream. If only he could see his father again. So often he thought about that last wonderful day they'd had together: Apu's arm close around him on the train home, telling him the story of the White Stag.

There was a sudden crackling in the bushes behind him, and he caught a glimpse of white. His heart jumped.

Then Bandi, the youngest of their Scout troop, darted out into the opening, the white numbers on his cap reflecting the late afternoon sun. He stood for a moment, frowning and looking around.

"Hey!" Stephen said.

Bandi ducked behind a boulder, looking flustered. Stephen stood up. "It's all right, Bandi. I'm out of the game already. Pali surprised me a few minutes ago."

Bandi looked relieved. "Where's Dini? Maybe I can find him and call his number."

Stephen laughed. "Do you expect me to tell you? Dini's on my team, remember?" Bandi looked so disappointed, Stephen relented. "Try that stand of alder trees." He pointed. "But you'd better hurry. Pali headed that way a few minutes ago."

A shout from the top of the hill.

Stephen looked up. It was Pali hurrying toward them, pointing back over his shoulder. Stephen frowned. What was going on? Then he saw the shadow of the man marching stiffly behind Pali, and a chill ran up his back.

"AVO!" he whispered.

He grabbed his numbered cap and shoved it into his pocket. Bandi's hands shook as he did the same. They stood and waited while Pali walked toward them, followed by the officer. Stephen stared at the man's boots, still shiny, though damp leaves clung to the toe of one.

Those same boots, eight years ago. The two AVO officers standing over his father, and that shiny red line trickling down Apu's cheek.

Stephen clenched his fists. The AVO were Hungarians, too. How could they betray their own people this way?

Stephen felt a touch on his shoulder. George, his brother-in-law. Their unofficial Scout leader. If the AVO officer discovered they were a Scout troop, George could be arrested.

16

Scouting was forbidden by the Communist Party.

"What are you doing here?" the AVO officer demanded.

Stephen felt George's hand tighten on his shoulder, but his voice sounded normal as he answered. "We're on an outing. These are students from my science study group."

The expression on the officer's face didn't change. He jabbed a finger in George's direction. "Your name and position." It was a command rather than a question.

"George Magas. I teach at the Technical University."

"Let me see your identification—all of you." Stephen's hand fumbled to his inside jacket pocket.

The Scout cap! He poked it farther down into the pocket. The officer watched as Stephen felt for the red booklet, his fingers clumsy. The AVO accepted no excuses. These days, people disappeared from Hungary for less than this. Like his father.

Stephen's stomach knotted. Finally his hand closed around the booklet, and he pulled it out.

"How long will you be here?" the officer asked, looking through the booklets.

"We must have the boats back by tomorrow afternoon," George answered.

The AVO officer glared at George and handed back their papers. "See that you do. And if you make a campfire, be sure it's put out properly." He turned abruptly and walked back toward the top of the hill. Stephen stood stiffly, waiting, until the man was out of sight over the rise.

Then he sank down on the log. He hated this—always watching, afraid of being caught.

How long would they have to live this way?

Chapter 2
A Capitalistic Otter

Pali spat on the ground. "Pig! Who does he think he is? We're not his slaves."

Bandi's face was so pale his freckles looked painted on. He sat down beside Stephen. "Now what, George? Do we have to go home?"

"I don't think he'll be back. Let's go ahead and get camp set up."

Stephen stood up, despite his trembling legs, and started along the trail toward the camp clearing. He heard Pali behind him, still muttering. It seemed Pali was always angry lately, even when things went well.

"Hey!" Dini came from the clearing, walking toward them on the trail. "What's taking you so long? The *gulyás* is ready to eat. Come and get it."

George walked over to him. "You missed out on our little adventure."

"I saw what was happening, but the officer didn't see me, so I scurried back to get dinner ready."

Stephen let out a shaky breath. "Dini, doesn't anything frighten you?"

Dini shrugged. "What good does it do to worry? Come on. Eat some of my good stew. I put lots of onions and paprika in it."

Stephen shook his head. But he, along with the others, followed Dini back to the clearing. He washed up, then helped himself to a bowl of the savory-smelling *gulyás*.

"I'm sick of this," Pali said. "The AVO, always looking for someone to deport! Did you know they took Tibor yesterday? Right from his stand on József Boulevard. What could they want with old Tibor, selling his cones of chestnuts? *He's* no landowner!" He paced back and forth, his bowl in his hand.

"Would they deport us if they found out we were Scouts?" Bandi asked.

George nodded. "It's possible. Certainly they would arrest me, your leader."

"But why is Scouting illegal?"

Pali glowered. "The Soviets can't stomach any organized group *they* don't control. I've had it! Things have got to change, and soon."

Dini helped himself to a second bowl of *gulyás*. "What about the meeting George and Stephen went to last week? There were Communists there, right? Some of them want changes, too."

Pali shook his head impatiently. "Meetings! Meetings aren't going to change anything! We need a revolution. The Hungarian people must—"

A sharp crackle in the bushes. Pali stopped in the middle of his sentence.

Stephen's stomach went cold. Had the AVO returned? George stood up and walked slowly over to the bushes. Stephen held his breath. They should keep talking. He tried to think of something to say, something safe. His mind felt numb.

They waited. The red light from the flames cast flickering shadows. The only sound was the crackling of the fire.

George let out a whoop and they all jumped. A loud rustling came from the bushes, then the sound of a distant splash. George pushed a shrubby branch aside and stepped back into their circle. He was smiling. "It was only a *vidra*, and I do not think this otter was a Communist. He looked quite capitalistic to me."

Stephen let out a shaky breath, and even Pali laughed. "All right, Stephen. Tell us about the meeting. But don't blather."

They huddled close to the fire; Stephen found himself speaking in a whisper. "There *were* Communists at the meeting; the writers challenged them. They told them that, according to Marxist teaching, they're not acting like true Communists—that they should reform."

Pali snorted. "And what did our comrades do? Did they confess and promise to do better?" He poked the fire vehemently. "I won't work on a collective farm! I want my own land, like my father had before the Communists took it."

Stephen shoved his hands into his pockets. "Quit complaining, Pali. Your land! At least you still have your father!" He jumped to his feet. "I'm going for a walk."

Blindly he shoved his way through bushes and tree branches that tore at his jacket. Soon he reached the grassy area near the beach. He stood silently until the churning in his stomach stopped.

He sat down on a rock. It still felt warm though the sun had set over an hour ago. Above him the stars flickered, bits of broken glass in the dark velvet sky.

He shifted; his boots crunched against the gravelly beach.

His boots. They had belonged to his father; now they fit him. It was hard to believe eight years had passed since he had seen Apu.

Off in the distance, a train wound its slow way, a pencil line against the deepening dusk. Had his father been taken away on a train like that one? Had he been crammed into a filthy boxcar with other unlucky "insects" who had been arrested?

Stephen sighed and looked out across the twinkling lights of Budapest just beyond the broad expanse of the Danube that flowed into the darkness. Strains of "The Blue Danube Waltz" rippled through his mind. He moved his hands, picking out imaginary chords. That beautiful music, made for dance. But tonight the Danube did not dance. It lay heavily before him like a strip of metal.

The blue Danube.

Tonight it was black.

Chapter 3
Ready to Fight

Tuesday, October 23, 1956

Stephen shifted at his desk, trying to make room for his legs. He stared through the window to the street outside. Something was wrong.

A university student, breathing out puffs of steam in the cold October air, slipped a piece of paper into an old man's hand. The man looked around nervously, then pushed the flyer back. Stephen leaned forward. What could the paper say to upset the old man so much?

"Mister Kôváry!"

He jumped, cracking his knees against the top of the desk.

"I realize this may seem a waste of time to a would-be Beethoven such as you," his teacher growled. "But if you can spare the time, you might answer the question."

His heart raced. What had Mr. Tóth asked? He had no idea. He unfolded his cramped legs and stood up. Someone snickered behind him; his face felt hot. He knew without looking that it was Jóska Káldor.

Mr. Tóth paced back and forth in front of the class, stopping abruptly before the life-sized picture of Lenin. "Well, Stephen, since you seem to be at a loss about the question, I'll refresh your memory. Who was Kossuth?"

Stephen let out his breath. Every boy in his class could answer that question!

"Lajos Kossuth was the freedom fighter who led our people during the 1848 uprising."

The teacher nodded, and Stephen sat down. Dini, two rows closer to the door, wiggled his eyebrows and grinned. Stephen tried not to laugh. Dini reminded him of a good-natured performing bear.

Mr. Tóth was looking at him again. Stephen forced himself to listen. "Kossuth is just one of many. The people of Hungary have always had brave men to come forward in our time of need."

Stephen frowned. Where were those brave men now? He thought about their weekend outing on St. Endre Island.

That AVO man who had stumbled on them. His stomach tightened. For as long as he could remember, they'd all lived in terror of the secret police. Just the mention of AVO was enough to make any person look nervously behind him.

It was a good thing they'd had proper identification with them on Saturday.

His stomach rumbled, bringing him back to the present. Just a few more minutes until lunch. He felt the small package in his jacket pocket. Bread with lard again; he wished there were some meat to go with it.

He thought about his sister, Mária. What would happen when she had the baby in a few weeks? The food shortages were worse all the time—another gift of the Soviets!

How could Mr. Tóth stand here in front of them talking of freedom, and still be a Communist? It didn't make sense.

The bell shrilled, and several of the boys shuffled to their feet, heading out into the hall. Stephen stood up and motioned to Dini. His mouth watered as he noticed a piece of *bukta* on the corner of Dini's desk; he could almost taste the tart plum filling. Dini took a huge bite of the pastry and nodded that he was willing to share.

Just as he reached Dini's desk, Jóska Káldor pushed by them, nearly knocking Stephen over in his hurry to get to the teacher's desk. "Mr. Tóth, I have something to ask you."

Stephen frowned. Jóska's father was with the AVO. "Listen to him, Dini," he whispered. "Which one of us will he tell on today?" He felt a familiar anger rising in his chest.

Jóska laid a stack of papers on the teacher's desk. "Here are my assignments. I want to ask you about my chances of going to the university in Moscow when I finish here." Mr. Tóth glanced at the top paper. "It shouldn't be hard for you to get in, Jóska. Your grades are satisfactory."

Stephen slammed his fist on Dini's desk, nearly knocking the remaining *bukta* to the floor.

Mr. Tóth looked over, and Dini stood up, brushing crumbs from his mouth. "Sorry, Mr. Tóth. I dropped my book." He lowered his voice. "Stephen, come out into the hall before your temper gets us both in trouble."

"Satisfactory grades!" Stephen nursed his aching hand. "That's because I tutor him. Jóska has the brain of a gnat!"

Dini grabbed Stephen's arm and pulled him out into the hall. "Easy. You're getting too upset for your own good."

Stephen took an angry bite from the *bukta* Dini handed

him. "If Jóska gets to Moscow, it's because of his father, and for no other reason."

"So what, Stephen? Let it go."

"What about us, Dini, when we finish here? You want to go to medical school, like your uncle did. Do you think you have a chance?"

Dini took another bite of *bukta*. "I'm willing to wait and find out."

Stephen snorted. "Your father refused to join the Communist Party before he died; you'll pay for that." He paced back and forth in the hall. "And I won't get into the Music Academy either. It's not fair."

"You're good, too," Dini said. "That piano piece you composed for your grandmother's birthday—it made her cry. She said it was as good as a Liszt rhapsody."

Stephen held back a smile. "I'm not *that* good." He sighed. "Not that it would matter. There's no way they'd let me into the Academy. My father owned too much land before . . . before they took him away."

That autumn night. Stephen would never forget the sight of his mother standing in the doorway, knuckles pressed to her mouth, as Apu was snatched away from them.

Anger hardened inside him. "I'm sick of the AVO and all they stand for. Even on our weekend trip, one of them had to show up!"

"Why be so upset, Stephen? He questioned you and left."

"What about Bandi? His first Scout outing, and this happens. Did you see his face afterward? He was terrified." Stephen folded his arms. "Maybe Pali's right when he says we should revolt."

"Bandi will be all right. He'll understand now why our

Scout troop has to be secret. And Pali? Pali's always ready to revolt. Look at him now; he's up to something." Dini pointed toward the schoolyard.

Pali, his face sweating with excitement, pushed through a crowd of boys standing by the doorway. "Stephen! Dini! I told you the time would come."

Stephen stared at the paper Pali waved in front of them. "What are you talking about? What have you got?"

"Your brother-in-law, George, just gave this to me. He looked for you but couldn't wait. These flyers are being passed out all over the city at this very moment."

The same flyer he'd seen the student handing out a few minutes ago.

Before he could get a good look, the bell shrilled and boys crowded into the hall. Pali shoved his way into their midst and held up the flyer. "Quick! I have something to read—something that will change all of our lives." He strode back into the classroom. Most of the boys followed.

Stephen pushed down his resentment. How did Pali do this? People always paid attention to him.

Pali marched up to Mr. Tóth, showed him the flyer, and said something in a low voice. The teacher nodded.

Stephen stared. Would Antal Tóth allow this to be read in the class?

Pali waited while the last of the students shuffled back into the classroom. Then he read loudly from the printed page in his hand.

"We, the workers, peasants, and students of our country, demand the withdrawal of Soviet troops from Hungary in accordance with the peace treaties."

Whispers stopped. There was silence.

*"We demand free elections, freedom of religion, freedom of
the press, freedom of assembly . . . "*

As Pali read the demands—sixteen in all—Stephen's
heart hammered. He felt as if he were listening from far
away, and yet Pali's words rang in his ears.

If they were free, really free, he could go to the Music
Academy after all to be a conductor and composer.

And there would be no food shortages; he wouldn't be
hungry all the time.

He remembered that last time he and Mária had been at
their country home when he was small. They'd hidden in
the hayloft, giggling, and collected eggs from the chickens.
And that night they'd had a fine meal of chicken *paprikash*
and noodles, with a chocolate-cream layered *dobos* cake for
dessert.

So much food; it made him hungry just to think of it. But
that was before . . . before Apu had been taken. It seemed
like another lifetime.

Pali finished reading. His look was fierce, daring anyone
to disagree with what he'd just read. The boy sitting next to
Stephen yelled out suddenly, "We'll *fight* for freedom if we
must!"

The spell was broken. The class yelled and stomped their
feet. But Jóska Káldor's face was white as he stood by Mr.
Tóth's desk.

Stephen's hands felt cold. He was surprised at how afraid
he felt. He wanted freedom, yes. That's what his father had
wanted, too.

But look at the price his father had paid. He wiped his damp hands on his pants. Why was Mr. Tóth allowing this shouting about freedom? He was a Communist.

Finally, Pali raised his arm for silence. "Our brothers in Poland held protests for freedom this week. To show our support, it is planned that we march to the statue of Bem and read the Sixteen Points to all the people."

Bem, the Polish leader who had fought along with Kossuth.

The shouting started again. The boy across the aisle pulled out colored pencils and hastily sketched a Kossuth emblem—that symbolic version of Hungary's rivers and mountains with the apostolic cross in the background. He tore it out and stuck it on his shirt. Several others did the same, and then pushed their way out of the classroom, bumping into one another and yelling.

Pali swaggered over to him. "Are you going to sit there all day?"

Stephen jumped to his feet. "I'm as ready to fight for freedom as you are, Pali!" He pulled a sheet of paper out of his desk and drew the Kossuth symbol. He pinned it to his shirt, hoping Pali wouldn't notice his shaking hands. "Let's go."

When they left the classroom, Stephen took a quick look back.

Only Mr. Tóth and Jóska still stood there.

Chapter 4
The First Shot

Stephen followed Pali down the stairs. Outside in the street, clumps of students rushed by, all talking at once. A yellow streetcar clattered past, jammed with dozens of people. Someone in the back of the tram tossed a handful of leaflets, which showered to the ground. Stephen stepped off the curb to grab one, but a young man pushed by, almost knocking him down. Pali jerked him back next to the building. Stephen rubbed his arm. "I can't believe it. Look at all these people. Nobody seems afraid."

"George wants us to meet him by his office. Come on." Pali squeezed past a group of young women who were handing out more leaflets. Stephen hurried to keep up with him.

On their right was a factory. As he and Pali passed it, dozens of workers streamed out the doors. Stephen stared. "They're laughing. How long has it been since we've heard laughing on the streets?"

"The Soviets can't ignore us now. Your brother-in-law has

done a good job. He and the others at the university have been passing out copies of the Sixteen Points all over the city."

Stephen shook his head. "The first time Mária brought George home to meet us, he was so quiet. I can't believe he'd do something like this!"

"Well, he did. Now, if only a little of his courage could rub off on you!"

Stephen glared at him, but Pali kept talking. "We've been lucky with George as our scout leader. If this goes well, our troop won't have to be secret any longer."

"Quiet, Pali!" Stephen lowered his voice. "You don't know who's listening, and you know what the Soviets do to those who cause trouble."

That night.

That black car pulling away from the curb with Apu in it. His sister's sobs all through that long night, fading as she dozed, beginning again each time she awakened.

Stephen's stomach tightened.

He and Pali crossed the bridge from Pest. They were in Buda now. There were more people on the street here, clusters of students and factory workers joining each other, forming larger groups, walking arm in arm through the streets. Stephen searched the crowd, looking for George. It wasn't far to his office at the university.

There, he saw him now. Mária was with him. She shouldn't be here; it was only two weeks before the baby was due. What if she got hurt in the crowd?

George signaled them over. Stephen pushed through a group of students and stooped to hug Mária. "What are you doing here, Mária? I thought you stayed home from the university today."

"I'll go back home soon, but I had to come and see for myself. Isn't this wonderful? We're finally standing up against the Soviets."

"I'm surprised Grandmother let you come."

Mária's eyes sparkled. "I told her I was going out to get bread."

George shook his head. "What am I going to do with this sister of yours, Stephen?" He moved to her side as a group of laughing students shoved by them, but not quickly enough. A stray elbow poked her in the stomach, and she winced.

George put a protecting arm around her shoulder. "Come, Mária, I'll take you home. It's getting too crowded here for safety."

The two of them started off down the street. Pali frowned. "If I had a sister, Stephen, I wouldn't be as soft with her as you are with Mária. You and George treat her as if she were a child."

"Mária has a mind of her own. She wouldn't go home even now if she didn't want to." He watched as the two disappeared into the crowd.

Someone pushed from behind, and Stephen took a quick step forward to keep from falling. The crowd almost filled the street now. He couldn't believe how quickly it had grown.

He kept moving, Pali beside him, as they inched along toward the Square, where the statue of Bem stood. Someone in front of him began to sing loudly the Kossuth nóta, that old song of Hungarian freedom, and Stephen joined in along with several others. He was surprised at how strong their voices sounded together. It brought tears to his eyes.

He didn't care who saw his tears. This was a moment like no other. Even Pali sang, a proud look on his face. They were almost to the Square. People elbowed one another, trying to get as close to the statue as possible. Was Anyu home by now? He felt a flicker of worry but pushed it down. His mother could take care of herself in almost any situation. She'd had to since Apu had been taken away.

The man in front of him shouted, "The flag! We want the old Hungarian flag!" A gray-haired woman leaned over the balcony above Stephen and dropped down the flag that hung there. She reminded him of Grandmother with her dried-apple cheeks. The man picked up the flag from the ground.

"Pah!" He spat. "This is not our Hungarian flag. The Soviets have ruined it with that red star of theirs!"

"We can change that," Pali said. "Stephen, give me your pocketknife." Stephen held the knife for a moment before handing it to Pali. The casing was burnished with age, but the blade was still true.

Apu's knife. Anyu had given it to Stephen on his twelfth birthday.

Pali poked the sharp point into the flag and pulled at the material in the center. The workers cheered. In place of the hated red star there was now a jagged hole.

The man next to him laughed. "If only we could get rid of the Soviets as easily as we get rid of their red star!"

"It may not be easy, but this time we will do it!" Pali muttered.

The statue of Bem towered above them. Stephen could

see the familiar plumed hat, the heroic stance of this man who meant so much to both the Hungarian and the Polish people.

The crowd fell silent. Stephen craned his neck to see. Beneath the statue a young man stood, his eyes dark with emotion. When he spoke, his voice sounded sharp in the silence.

"Let us rise! Our country calls us!
Now or never! Time enthralls us.
Shall we live as slaves or freemen?
These the questions. Choose between them!"

The back of Stephen's neck prickled. These were the poet Petôfi's words—the same words that had ignited the 1848 revolution.

The crowd, stretching back as far as Stephen could see, shouted out the last few lines of the poem.

"By the God of every Magyar
Do we swear
Do we swear the tyrant's handcuffs
Not to bear!"

Stephen's ears rang as the words echoed against the walls of the old buildings, bouncing back in a deafening wave of sound.

The tyrant's handcuffs. His father knew about tyrant's handcuffs.

The crowd moved slowly across the bridge, back toward the Parliament building. Stephen saw Dini edging his way toward them. How had he ever found them?

He wondered where Jóska Káldor was now. Still standing palefaced in the classroom with Mr. Tóth? Or out hunting for his AVO father to see what to do next?

All around him people were chanting, singing, repeating Petőfi's words. The noise pressed against Stephen in waves. His mind churned. What would it mean, to be free?

Free to be a musician instead of spending his life working in a factory?

Free to see Mária's baby grow up without fear—the fear that at any moment someone you loved might be arrested and dragged out of your life forever?

Free! Free! Free! The words drummed in his mind, keeping rhythm with the chanting of the crowd, as they waited now in front of the Parliament building.

"Stephen!"

Dini shook him. "Are you all right?" Dini's cheeks were red with excitement. "That was Imre Nagy who just spoke. Did you recognize him? My uncle says he's our hope. If the Communist party puts him back in power, maybe we can achieve freedom without a fight."

Pali shook his head. "It won't work. We'll have to fight. Gerő's on the radio right now, denouncing us. As Party Secretary, he's the one with the power; Imre Nagy hasn't a chance!" Pali pushed closer to the speakers blasting out Gerő's voice.

The crowd began to shout. "Down with Gerő. To the Radio building! We will read the Sixteen Points to all of Hungary."

Stephen moved slowly down Alkotmány Street, packed so tightly in the crowd now he felt like a cog in some gigantic machine. At the edge of the crowd someone rolled a newspaper, lit it, held it aloft. The torch burned sullenly in the late afternoon dusk, then burst into brightness.

As it did, Stephen felt the change of mood in the crowd. Energy surged around him.

It reminded him of a time when he was a child, sitting on Apu's shoulders on top of Gellért Hill. He'd shouted into the wind, feeling taller than the world, so powerful.

But now, instead of Apu, it was Pali's face he saw, looking fierce in the flickering light of the torches. "This time we'll gain our freedom! I will live on my own land again."

A few more minutes, and the gray Radio Building loomed ahead down narrow Bródy Sándor Street. Stephen could make out two AVO men in the window of the building. The crowd pushed forward, filling the narrow street. More AVO officers leaned out the upper windows of the Radio Building. They held submachine guns in their hands, the dreaded "davay guitars."

His excitement drained away. The crowd seemed edgy now. People around him grumbled, trying to shift position. Someone from up front shouted back a message. "Our committee is inside. They will broadcast the Sixteen Points."

"I'll believe that when I hear it," Pali muttered. Stephen was jammed in with people on all sides now, but Pali somehow worked his way forward to the very front of the crowd. Stephen saw him speak to a young woman who struggled to stay standing as people pushed her from behind.

She stood by the massive wooden gates; it sounded as if the crowd was trying to break through. AVO officers barred the way, holding their guns in position.

The streetlights burned brightly in the dark. Stephen's hands felt clammy; he rubbed them together to warm them. He thought of Anyu, and of Mária and Grandmother. Were they safe?

The crowd shifted, and a stout merchant woman pushed up against Stephen. "Why is it taking so long?" she demanded. Her butcher's apron was bloody from her day's work. He tried to pull back, but couldn't. The sound of scuffling and muffled shouts came from the front of the crowd. His eyes and throat began to burn, and thick clouds of acrid smoke billowed up.

Dini swore. "What are they doing now?"

Stephen pulled out his handkerchief and wiped his streaming eyes. The pushing was worse. He felt his rib cage crushed between Dini and the woman with the bloody apron. The smell of it made him feel sick. He tried to shift position; the sharp elbow of the man beside him caught him in the ribs.

Pali was still talking to the young woman; she looked like she was crying. The crowd pushed forward.

The girl stumbled and almost fell to the pavement. Pali grabbed her and pulled her back to her feet. Stephen saw the look of fury on the guard's face. His heart began to race. The crowd surged forward. He heard the sound of splintering wood.

The guard fired. Stephen saw the winking dot of red light, then heard screams.

More firing. The windows and roof of the Radio Building were suddenly alive with AVO officers.

Next to him, the butcher woman began to sob. "My God, my God—No, it cannot be."

The girl fell to the ground. Stephen caught one glimpse of her blood-covered face, her blonde hair staining red as she fell.

The Revolution had begun.

Chapter 5
The Hands of a Killer?

He stood stunned for a moment, unable to believe what was happening. The man next to him lurched forward, and Stephen stumbled. He fell against the butcher woman, then caught himself.

More shouting. A sudden blast of water hit him, knocking him backward.

Fire hoses.

People ran in all directions, screaming, trying to get away from the force of the water. He pushed his way toward the edge of the crowd, slipping on wet cobblestones.

He saw the construction site then, stacks of boards and bricks just ahead. Others were there already, snatching bricks to pitch at security guards. A volley of shots rang out as the guards fired wildly into the crowd.

Stephen sprinted toward a pile of planks.

A crackling sound from above.

The man next to him slumped to the ground. Stephen felt himself jerked back. "Down, you idiot!" It was Pali, grasping his collar. "Here. Take this." Pali thrust something toward him in the shadowy darkness. Stephen felt the cold metal in his hands. "It's loaded," Pali said. "Use it!"

Stephen hunched over, unable to believe he was holding a gun. It seemed to vibrate in his hands.

A machine-gun rattled from the roof. He dove behind the pile of boards. An AVO command car had been torched at the corner; the thick smoke and rubbery stench made his eyes water. He wiped them on his sleeve and huddled behind a construction pile. The flames from the burning car shot higher, orange and red licking the sky, silhouetting the shadows of running people. Footsteps, shouts, gunshots echoed from the walls of the buildings.

Another volley of shots ricocheted from the roof of the Radio Building. Pali cursed, braced his gun against the stack of wood, and fired toward the guards.

Stephen's fingers were slippery with sweat as he clutched the gun to his chest. He couldn't do it. He couldn't shoot.

He couldn't kill.

From the corner of his eye, he saw Dini dragging the body of a young woman toward a nearby pile of bricks. Was she dead? A little girl, no more than three or four, toddled after them. What in God's name was she doing here? "Mama," she called out. Dini swore and grabbed for the child, pulling her to the ground just as the AVO bullet whined by his shoulder.

No time to think. The officer was just yards away, firing at Dini. Dini, who had no gun!

Stephen stood up, took a step. He saw the fury that twisted the AVO officer's face as the man lifted his gun to shoot. There was a roaring in Stephen's ears.

He raised his own gun, pointed. He was surprised at how light it felt now, warm in his hands, seeming to move into position by itself.

He fired. The gun jerked against his shoulder. He saw the surprised look on the officer's face as the bullet hit. The man's body shuddered and fell. He lay crumpled on the ground a few feet away.

Stephen took a step forward and looked down unbelievingly. The moonlight glinted on the chain around the man's neck. A cross? No, it couldn't be.

The man was dead. Even in the dark Stephen could tell. He shut his eyes tight, swallowing down a wave of nausea. A jerk on his arm. It was Pali.

"Stephen! We've got to get out of here."

"The little girl," he said, looking around for her. His voice felt thick.

"Dini has her," Pali said. "She's all right. Come on!" Stephen looked down at the gun in his hands.

"Stephen!" Pali hissed again. "The armory. Come on. We need more guns." Pali sprinted toward the corner. Stephen followed. At the corner he stopped again, staring down at his hands.

There was no blood. He had killed a man, but there was no blood on his hands.

Sometimes, when he played the piano, he'd watch his fingers, amazed at the miracle of music. He could make others laugh or cry, simply by touching the keys of the piano.

He had the hands of a musician, his grandmother said.

Now, with these hands, he had killed a man.

Chapter 6
Molotov Cocktails

Wednesday, October 24

It was almost noon, fourteen hours since that first shot had been fired last night at the Radio Building. Stephen paused by the corner of the apartment building. He had to get back to his own house to see if Anyu and Mária had made it home safely. He set the heavy bag of food down and wiped sweat from his face, surprised at the soot that came off with it.

So many fires still burning. He leaned against the old brick wall of the building, feeling its coolness against his back. He was tired.

Fourteen hours. It seemed more like days. In those hours he'd killed a man. Perhaps others. It had been hard to tell in the confusion, in the shadowy darkness of the night fighting.

He looked down at the submachine gun slung across his chest like a guitar. He picked up the heavy bag of food again. It was better not to think. There was no use regretting what had happened.

When he'd left Pali a few minutes ago, he and others were hastily building a barricade of park benches and paving stones—anything to stop the Soviet tanks that patrolled the streets.

The tanks had come in before dawn, shooting at every moving target—and some that were not. He heard the rattle of machine-guns now, coming from the area by Corvin Cinema.

He looked around. A gaping hole was torn through the front walls of the corner bakery; the blackened counter inside still smoldered. What would Mrs. Beke do now? She had supported her family with her salary from this bakery all these years since her husband had been taken.

A burned-out car lay tipped on its side just ahead of him. As he edged around it, holding his heavy bag, he tripped over something and looked down. A young man, not much older than he, lay dead at his feet. He bent down to take a closer look.

It was the boy who helped out at the butcher shop. His dark hair was matted with blood that oozed from some unseen wound.

Stephen swallowed down the sickness that rose in his throat. He took a crumpled handkerchief from his pocket and covered the face, the vacant eyes. Was this how the AVO officer had looked last night when Stephen shot him? He had tried not to look at the face.

Last night didn't seem real. None of this did.

A tank rumbled down the street, and Stephen ducked behind the side of the building. Two Soviet soldiers peered out of the turret opening as the tank rolled past. The one, with his dark curly hair, looked like Dini.

Where was Dini now? The last he'd seen him, he was kneeling in the middle of the street by the Radio Building, helping his uncle tend to the wounded. That had been hours ago. Stephen couldn't stop thinking of the look on Dini's face after he'd taken the little girl to her grandmother's house—the little girl whose mother had died.

Dini, his carefree friend, whose greatest concern until last night was keeping his belly full.

The tank turned onto Üllôi Street. Stephen waited a few moments longer, then edged out of his hiding place. The bag banged heavily against his side, but he couldn't leave it. They'd need food in the days to come.

He stumbled again on the rough pavement as he turned onto József Boulevard. He squinted in the smoky haze, straining to see their apartment building. Was it still standing?

Yes! His tense muscles relaxed.

The apartment across the street had burned. It looked like a skull, glowing red inside. Bandi's cousins lived in that building— where were they now?

He thought of Anyu and Mária and Grandmother. Please, let them be safe.

He ducked through the doorway of his house into the entry hall. It was quiet, too quiet. For a moment he panicked.

He remembered then, and let out a shaky breath. Of course. They wouldn't be upstairs, in the apartments. They would all be down in the cellar to escape the artillery.

He'd been just a toddler when the Soviets had marched into Budapest at the end of the war, but he had vague memories of the chilly dark cellar and the smell of potato-

43

onion soup cooking on the iron stove.

And his father's stories about the White Stag.

He remembered sitting on Apu's lap, listening to the stories and staring up at a long crack in the ceiling. The crack seemed to change shape with each story: sometimes it was a river, sometimes a road, sometimes a flash of lightning in a fierce storm.

Stephen shook his head. He didn't have time now to think of that, to remember the pain after Apu was taken and there were no more stories.

The heavy door that led down to the cellar banged as Stephen swung it open. There was silence below. The walls, as he started down, felt damp and cold, and cobwebs hung in the corners. He dragged the bag of food down the steps, each thump loud in the silence. He could see the dim shapes of the furniture—empty chairs, tables, beds with carved wooden headboards, all piled together in corners, stored for friends who had been deported.

"Stephen!" His mother's face was pale in the dim light, and he let out a sigh of relief. She was all right.

"Thank God it's you!" She hurried over to him, hugged him. He rested his head for a moment on her shoulder, strands of her blonde hair brushing against his cheek.

His eyes adjusted to the shadows now. He saw Mária and Grandmother seated at the table, with a large pan and bottles of tomato sauce in front of them. He puzzled over this. What were they cooking?

Then he saw the can of gasoline on the floor, and he knew. Molotov cocktails.

They were emptying out the tomato sauce, filling the bottles with gasoline, using rags for wicks.

Mária pushed back her chair and struggled to her feet, her stomach bulging under the apron she had tied around her. "We were worried, Stephen."

His grandmother frowned at him, but he saw the relief in her eyes. "You should have come back sooner, if only to get something to eat." She walked heavily over to him. He smelled the faint scent of lilacs mixed with the pungent odor of the gasoline as she kissed him, first on one cheek and then the other.

"I have eaten, Grandmother. I had fresh milk and some bread, and I've brought food back as well, given to us by farmers from Vecsés and Monor." He opened the bag, took out several loaves of bread, then the long fat *tök*. He laid the squash on the shelf above the stove. "Have you heard the news? Imre Nagy is now our Prime Minister."

His grandmother crossed her arms angrily over her dark shawl. "I don't think we can trust him! On the radio they say it is Nagy who brought in the Soviet tanks."

"I do not believe that," Anyu said. "There were Russian tanks in the city by four o'clock this morning—just hours after the shooting at the Radio Building. The Soviets planned this. They allowed Imre Nagy to take over as Prime Minister for one reason only: to have a scapegoat."

She swayed then, and Stephen saw the exhaustion in her eyes. "I'm all right," she said. "Only a little tired. But I need to go back to the office soon. The freedom fighters are using the Telex there to try to get messages out to the West." She looked up at him. "I don't have much hope for this, Stephen. The Soviets are merciless; you saw what they did to your father, dragging him away. And who knows where he is now—if he is still alive."

Could his father still be alive? Stephen's throat was tight, remembering how Apu used to sit with him each night after supper, teaching him to carve with his pocketknife. The smell of the pine wood, the sawdust shavings making him sneeze. The warm feel of Apu's wool sweater against his cheek as he guided Stephen's small hand with his big one.

For the first time in these eight years, Stephen felt a flicker of hope. If they could win this fight for freedom, he might see his father again. He put his arm around his mother's shoulder. "We'll make the Soviets leave, Anyu. This morning, Pali and I stopped a tank with Molotov cocktails. That's just two of us. There are thousands of our men out fighting right now."

"Men! They're boys, Stephen. Many of them are younger than you." Anyu's eyes welled up with tears. "An hour ago I bandaged the wounds of a twelve-year-old carrying a rifle as tall as himself. He insisted on going back out to fight as soon as I finished."

His grandmother stomped back to the table. "Well then, he and the others will not fight unarmed." Her gray eyes were bright with anger. "Mária, empty the rest of the tomato sauce into that big pan. We will need more bottles for the Molotov cocktails."

Stephen sat down on the edge of the bed, his legs trembling with tiredness. "You must sleep," Anyu said. "You have been out all night. Here, I will help you with your boots." Stephen saw the look on her face as she tugged. She was remembering these boots.

His father's boots.

But he was too tired to think anymore. He lay down and, within moments, slept.

Chapter 7
The Parliament Massacre

Thursday, October 25

Early the next morning Stephen climbed the cellar stairs and stepped outside. He drew in a deep breath. The streets were empty now, except for piles of paving stones and streetcar barricades. The asphalt glistened with the rain that had fallen during the night. A fresh breeze lifted the edges of the red, white, and green flags that hung on the front of the apartment buildings.

His mother had been so angry when the Soviets put their red star in the flag's center. Now that hated star was gone—at least here. With knives, with anything sharp they could find, the Hungarian people had cut the center from all these flags.

Stephen's head ached. He'd slept restlessly, waking to the sound of gunfire. Soviet tanks, firing on Kilián Barracks, just a few blocks away. All night they'd kept up the barrage.

He was glad for the morning silence as he walked down

the back streets to Rákóczi Street. Perhaps one of the shops would be open, and he could get a crusty loaf of fresh bread for their breakfast. Strange to be thinking of food for his stomach. Yesterday he had killed a man.

And now he knew if he had to, he would kill again. He had a small pistol in his jacket pocket. It had been given to him yesterday by a Hungarian soldier; its cold weight bumped against his chest as he walked.

He still had his submachine gun, too, back in the cellar. When Pali had handed him that gun two nights ago, he didn't think he could use it.

But he had.

He thought now of Apu. If there was a chance that his father was still alive, that he could be freed, Stephen would fight, would even kill again.

But could Apu be alive after all these years? Stephen turned onto Tanács Boulevard.

Voices. Murmuring voices and shuffling feet.

He looked up. A large crowd moved slowly down the street toward him: Mothers with small children, some older women with dark kerchiefs tied under their chins, a few men. No guns, but many flags.

Stephen stepped back to make room for them to pass. A young woman with a brightly colored kerchief tied over her hair walked in front of Stephen, her baby cradled in one arm. In her other hand she held a single flower, a red rose. For just a moment he smelled its sweetness. Then she was past him, and he smelled only the choking ashiness from yesterday's fires.

The older woman passing him now carried a black flag. She was weeping. Had her son been killed in the fighting?

On a sudden impulse he stepped into line behind her.

They were almost to the Square when he saw the Soviet tank in the road ahead. His shoulders tightened. The woman with the baby didn't hesitate. She walked up to the tank and stood there, looking up at the commander. Stephen felt for the pistol hidden inside his coat pocket.

"We are unarmed, on our way to the Parliament Building for a peaceful demonstration!" the woman with the baby shouted out in Russian.

The tank commander waved them on. Stephen stood there for a moment, surprised. The mood of the crowd relaxed. Three young boys shouted up to the Soviet soldiers on the tank across the street. The soldiers laughed and pulled them aboard.

The tightness in Stephen's shoulders eased as he moved on, walking beside the woman. The tank clattered slowly down the street, a Hungarian flag flying crookedly from its turret. He'd heard rumors that many of the younger Soviet soldiers were in sympathy with the Hungarian people, but this amazed him.

The sun broke through the clouds and shone on the torn flags that fluttered above the Parliament Building. He saw several Soviet tanks parked around the Square. Some of the older women began to shout, "*Ruszkik Haza!* Russians go home!" Again Stephen felt a prickle of fear, but the soldiers only lounged by their tanks. A few of them talked to the women, some trying out broken bits of Hungarian.

Right now the fighting of yesterday seemed like a bad dream. He walked over and stood by the young Russian tank commander, who sat in the grass beside a small tree, chewing on the stem of a flower. "We would go if they let us," the young soldier said. "We do not want to be here."

Stephen glanced into the young soldier's eyes. Dark brown, like George's—and that same sincere look. Stephen sat down beside him. The young soldier took out a worn photograph.

"Look." He pointed to the picture. "My son."

Stephen took the photograph and looked at the round baby. He smiled and nodded.

Everything was quiet except for the distant sounds of machine-gun fire and an occasional hand grenade. Perhaps the soldiers would leave, and Hungary could finally be free. Was it that simple? Stephen leaned back against the trunk of the small tree.

Shouting, behind him.

He turned.

The sharp crack of a rifle shot. He crouched to the ground. What was happening?

The bullet whined by, just a few feet from him. He dropped the picture. The smiling baby face looked up at him from the grass.

Another shot. The woman next to him fell. The wide-eyed little girl beside her dropped to the ground, clutching a ragged bit of satin blanket.

The rattle of machine-gun fire. Three more people fell.

The roof.

The roof of the Department of Agriculture, directly across from the Parliament Building, was alive with AVO men, firing into the crowd.

Stephen stood up. He tried to shout but his voice made no sound at all, covered over by the staccato clatter of machine-gun fire.

The Russian soldier next to him thrust his own gun into Stephen's hand, then leapt up onto his tank. "Behind my tank for shelter—shoot back!" he mouthed. He slammed the hatch shut. Moments later the tank turret swiveled, and the Soviet soldier fired at the security guards on the roof.

In a blur, Stephen saw the other Russian commander motion people behind his tank. He, too, had his turret gun trained on the roof. He closed his hatch and fired at the AVO hidden there.

But from the edge of the crowd came a thundering roar, and more people fell to the ground.

The Soviet tanks outside the Square were shooting into the crowd.

No time to think.

Stephen ducked behind the tank, rested his gun against a tread, fired at the roof.

The gun jerked in his hands. He fired again.

No feelings. He seemed to be watching a movie. A woman, weeping hysterically, knocked his arm as she crouched against the side of the tank while bullets rained around her. He reached to pull her behind the tank.

Too late. Her body shuddered as the bullet hit. Crimson drops sprayed from her chest.

She fell to the ground and lay there limply, like a rag doll tossed to the floor.

A white-haired man cursed and shook his fist at the police on the roof as he stumbled toward the tank.

The pistol. Stephen took it from his coat pocket, pushed it into the man's hand.

The movie jolted from frame to frame. People fell. Others trampled them. The little girl, still clutching her scrap of satin blanket, lay dead in the dirt just a few feet from him.

Bullets came from every side. The noise was deafening. Screaming, and the continual boom of tank fire. People forced their way into houses facing the square. Some squeezed into the hallways of the Parliament Building.

The old man knelt beside Stephen, muttering as he fired blindly toward the roof. A few freedom fighters raced into the Square now, arriving from surrounding neighborhoods. Side streets filled with the pounding of feet. Shouts, cries of pain tore open the afternoon.

Beethoven's *Emperor* Concerto. Giddily, Stephen thought of those musical sounds of war. He shook his head to clear it. This was no musical performance. This was real.

Smoke in the air. The sunshine turned hideous green. He choked, tried to suck in a breath. Squinted to see his targets on the roof.

An ambulance raced into the Square. The driver stopped, opened the door. People scrambled inside, pulling some of the wounded in with them.

The driver roared away.

Two more ambulances arrived. People clawed at the doors. The driver tried to pull as many aboard as possible. Bodies lay everywhere. Now Stephen shot blindly through the haze of smoke.

An ambulance screeched to a halt beside the tank. Dini leaned out.

"Stephen! Get in!"

He stood there, frozen. Dini grabbed his arm with a jerk. Stephen crawled into the back of the ambulance. The old man and two women climbed in after him. Stephen's head banged the side panel as Dini raced out of the Square. No pain. He didn't feel any pain.

Dini stopped a short distance down the side street.

"Out, all of you. I'm going back." Stephen stumbled out, the others behind him. Dini sped off again.

Someone, not far from where he stood, was calling out for help. He walked over and stood beside the young woman lying on the ground. The front of her blouse was stained dark with blood. One eye was swollen shut. Stephen looked down at her, wondering what had happened to her eye. A doctor hurried over. Stephen turned away.

Was it still the same day when Dini returned? George was with him. Stephen barely looked up; he was kneeling beside a boy with a bullet wound in his leg. Dini bent to help him, then he and George lifted the child into the ambulance. Stephen stood up.

Empty. He was a shell, with nothing left inside. A giant hand could pick him up and crush him easily.

Like the night his father had been taken. He'd leaned his cheek against the cold frame of his bed, lying awake all that night, it seemed. He did not cry. He felt dried up inside.

But even then, he had not felt as hollow as he did now.

"Stephen." George's voice was husky. "Colonel Pál Maléter needs freedom fighters to join his unit of the Hungarian Army at Kilián Barracks. Pali is there already; I'm going now. Do you want to come?"

Numb. He felt so numb. No energy to talk, to respond in any way.

George put his arm around his shoulder; Stephen didn't resist. Together they walked down Balassi Bálint Avenue.

They passed the Square. It was quiet now, roped off so no one could go in. There were trucks inside; Soviet soldiers piled bodies into them.

Something twisted inside Stephen. "They act as if they are loading pieces of wood." His breath caught in a shudder.

George's hand tightened on his arm. "Come, Stephen. We can do no good here now."

Chapter 8
The Café Rescue

Saturday, October 27

Stephen leaned against the Barracks window. He'd never felt this kind of tiredness before. Even when Kilián Barracks wasn't under siege, he couldn't rest; fragments of nightmares terrified him each time he dozed off.

A torn piece of satin blanket; a little girl's body.

The look of anguish on a dead woman's face.

And over and over, Apu, with a shiny trickle of blood running down his cheek.

He shifted his cramped legs. The shelling would start again any minute. The Soviets would not let up for long in their attack. But even Soviet tanks could not destroy the five-foot-thick walls of Kilián Barracks. It still stood, though many of the surrounding buildings were destroyed.

"How are you doing, Stephen?"

He jumped. He hadn't heard the footsteps behind him. "I just came from seeing Mária," George said. "She sends her

love. I think the baby will come sometime this week."
Stephen nodded. Soon he would be an uncle—if all went
well with Mária's baby.

Could anything go well in this world gone crazy?

He mustn't think this way. Mária had to be all right.

"Grandmother is there for the delivery," George said.
"Dini will help if he's needed. Your mother is still at the
Telex in the office."

Stephen didn't answer. Dini had returned yesterday to
the Barracks for medical supplies. He'd told Stephen about
the two babies he'd delivered since the fighting had started;
both babies had lived.

Stephen remembered the time when he and Dini had
been about ten and had gone with Grandmother to visit a
sick neighbor. The woman, Mrs. Kovács, went into sudden
labor, and Grandmother delivered the baby. Stephen had
been afraid. He'd waited in the corner of the room, not
wanting to watch. But Dini helped Grandmother, bringing
towels and other things she needed. Even then, Dini had
known he wanted to be a doctor.

"Stephen, are you sure you're all right?" George watched
him with concerned eyes.

"I'm all right."

But he wasn't, and he knew George could tell. The numbness he carried inside must show in his eyes.

George sat down on the cot beside him. "I've just heard
that freedom fighters found some of our political prisoners
here in the city and released them."

Stephen's heart jumped. Was it just one more rumor? If
Apu was alive, he'd be somewhere in one of those prisons.

Footsteps then, and a shadow in the doorway.

Pali.

"George! Colonel Maléter wants to see you."

Pali turned to Stephen. "You and I are to go to the Café Hungaria. AVO officers have trapped two freedom fighters on Dohány Street. Bandi's coming with us."

Here was Bandi now, standing behind Pali, ready for his chance to be part of the action. George walked over to him. "Bandi, does your mother know you're here at the Barracks?"

Bandi looked down. "She knows," he muttered.

She didn't know; Stephen was sure of that. Or if she did, she didn't want him here. George's voice was gentle. "As soon as this foray is finished, I want you to go home for a while. Do you understand?" He rested his hand for a moment on Bandi's shoulder. Bandi nodded, not looking up.

George handed Stephen his submachine gun. "Take care of yourself, Stephen." Maléter was in the doorway now, looking impatient. George turned to go with him.

The street was quiet outside the Barracks, but Stephen felt his stomach tighten. The tanks would return.

Pali looked up and down the street. "If we're careful, we can get across Rákóczi Avenue and then down to Dohány Street. That will be quickest. The fighting is right across from the Café Hungaria." They started out, single file, keeping close to the buildings. The day was cold, but Stephen felt a trickle of sweat edge its way down the back of his neck.

Six blocks down they nearly came face-to-face with four Soviet tanks. Stephen saw them first, parked on the side street. He jerked Pali back against the building and pointed to the telltale guns jutting out just above eye level.

Pali nodded. "We'll crawl past, single file," he whispered. "We need to get over to the other side of the street." They backtracked half a block, then crossed Rákóczi Avenue. A burned-out tram in the middle of the street shielded them from view. Pali moved silently from one pile of rubble to the next. Then Bandi, behind him, tripped over a loose paving stone. Pebbles rattled across the pavement.

Stephen stiffened; fear pricked his gut like broken glass. The Soviet soldier, standing beside his tank, jerked his head, staring right at them, it seemed. The soldier's submachine gun pointed their way as he searched for the source of the noise.

Stephen dared not move. Three women, dark kerchiefs wrapped around their hair, hurried out of the apartment building next to the soldier, carrying baskets to get bread. For just a moment the soldier turned to watch them. Pali held up his hand slightly. Stephen crept by the tanks to the next pile of rubble. Pali and Bandi followed like shadows behind him.

A sudden blast of gunfire; Stephen flattened himself against the ground. He raised his head cautiously. Just ahead, the outlines of the Café Hungaria rose from the smoky mist; the sulphurous smell of gunpowder hung in the air. In front of the Café, two young men lay motionless on the ground.

Dead. Stephen knew those vacant eyes.

Two other boys, not much older than Bandi, crouched behind a burned-out jeep near the building. AVO officers sprayed them with bullets from the roof of the apartment building.

Pali swore under his breath. "They're trapped. There's no

place for them to go."

Stephen scanned the street. "Two buildings down—the tobacco shop. The window's shattered."

"Let's go!" Pali was on his feet, zigzagging as he ran. Stephen, behind him, saw the blur of the two hand grenades as Pali threw them into the building where the snipers hid.

The crack of the explosion left Stephen's ears vibrating. He felt dizzy; nothing seemed clear. Sweat trickled into his eyes; he wiped it away as he ran.

He saw the two younger boys in front of him now, crouched behind the jeep. Stephen grabbed the gangly one by the shoulder. "Store front—two buildings down! Come on!" The boys jumped up as if attached to springs and ran, hunched over, pressing themselves against the building.

He saw the brick outline of the shop just in front of them. Bullets hit the ground by his feet. He threw himself over the low railing, vaguely aware of a blur of bodies as the other boys jumped beside him. He landed on the floor, banging his head against something sharp.

Ignoring the trickling wetness above his left eye, he pushed himself to his knees, ready to return fire. Bandi grabbed his arm. "Pali's hit!"

Pali hunched against a pile of rubble a few feet away, a perfect target for the tank just clanking into position. His face twisted with pain as he clutched his leg, blood oozing between his fingers.

Stephen hesitated only a moment, then stumbled back out over the window ledge. He grabbed Pali's shirt and tugged. Pali grunted, struggled to get up, still holding his bleeding leg. Stephen half-dragged, half-carried him the few feet back to the building.

The ping of bullets hit the wall beside them. Stephen strained to lift Pali over the ledge. With a quick jerk, Bandi pulled him to safety.

Stephen hoisted himself back over and dropped to the floor. Rifle fire ricocheted off the wall. An echoing boom, and most of the remaining wall crumbled to powder.

"Quick! The back room." He grabbed Pali's jacket, yanking him to safety.

The firing stopped. Stephen lay on the floor, struggling to catch his breath, while Bandi tore off a piece of shirt and wrapped it around Pali's leg. Pali winced as Bandi pressed against the wound to stop the blood flow. "Just a flesh wound," Bandi said.

Pali swore. He bit his lip as Bandi finished bandaging him.

Stephen sat up and took a sip from the *kulacs*. The metallic-tasting water felt cool as it trickled down his throat. He handed the canteen to Pali.

"You saved my life," Pali whispered hoarsely.

They were silent then, listening for the tanks. The boys they had rescued watched wide-eyed and tense until the tanks thundered away down the street, looking for bigger game.

Then the two boys slumped on the floor and slept. Stephen knew the kind of tiredness they felt, exhaustion that cared for nothing but sleep.

Pali looked at them. "Can you believe, Stephen, it was just a week ago George took us to the island for that secret Scout outing?"

Stephen sat silently. It seemed so long ago.

"I keep thinking about the *gulyás* Dini cooked—and that Scout game we played." Pali's voice was quiet. "I circled around behind you in the bushes, called out your number, and you were dead—and I won."

"I was angry at you because you were so much better than me at killing the enemy."

"Well, now we have both killed the enemy."

Stephen looked at him. "What do you think, Pali. Are we evil, too? These men we shoot—they have families. Some of them are barely older than we are."

Pali sat up, his eyes narrowed. "They made the choice. We didn't. We're only trying to defend our people and our country. We didn't attack *them*."

Stephen was quiet, remembering the young Russian soldier he'd talked to. For a moment he saw those dark brown eyes, so much like George's. He thought about the soldier's little boy, the chubby baby in the picture.

Something stirred inside him, something he couldn't explain.

"I saw that snake Jóska this morning," Pali said. "Down by the AVO headquarters, hunting for his traitor father."

"Four days, and he still hasn't found his father?"

"And who cares if he ever does? If his father knows what's good for him, he's cleared out of Hungary already. The AVO are finally starting to get what they deserve!" Pali scowled.

Stephen was silent.

Bandi shook his arm. "We have to get back to the Barracks before another tank comes. Pali, can you walk if we help you?" Pali nodded. He pushed himself into a sitting position. Stephen awakened the two sleeping boys. They seemed dazed, but scrambled to their feet.

Supporting Pali with his arm, Stephen made his way out behind the building, and they headed back to the Barracks.

Chapter 9
Searching for Apu

Saturday, October 27
late afternoon

Stephen stared down at the street, watching, struggling to stay awake. For the fragment of a dream he was small again, waiting at the apartment window for Apu to return home from the Department of Agriculture, to rub his tickly beard against Stephen's face, and toss him laughing into the air.

Then he jarred awake, and felt the cold stone ledge of the Barracks window beneath his arm. He looked back at Pali, asleep on the cot behind him.

He heard the rumbling sound then, getting louder. Two tanks clattered into sight.

The flash of gunfire.

The explosion shook the ground beneath him, and he dove to the floor. Easing into a fighting position, he raised his gun to the window and peered out cautiously.

At first he saw nothing but the dust and the smoke. Then, as it cleared, he saw the elderly man. He was trapped, his legs caught in a pile of debris from the explosion, struggling to free himself.

And in the third floor window in the building across from them was an AVO sniper. Stephen raised his gun, but the AVO pulled back, out of sight.

The old man called out for help, clawing at the chunks of concrete that held him. Stephen raced down the wide stone stairs of the Barracks to the first floor. He was outside then, blinking in the bright afternoon light, his eyes burning with the haze of smoke.

He ran to the old man, afraid to look up and see what the sniper was doing. A bullet whistled past his ear. Stephen's hands stung as he struggled with the chunks of stone that trapped the man. More bullets tore at the rubble; bits of cement flew into the air.

He grabbed a twisted piece of metal from the debris and jammed it under a slab of concrete to use as a lever. Sweat ran down his forehead, trickled into his eyes.

The tank. He saw it from the corner of his eye. The commander had spotted them and was turning, getting into position to fire.

He froze. Bandi, standing by the doorway of the Barracks, held up a Molotov cocktail, rushed out, and hurled it at the tank. A sudden flash, and the tank burst into flames. The cracked turret gun toppled and fell soundlessly, seeming to melt into the roaring flames.

Stephen grasped the old man beneath his armpits, struggling to stand in the uneven rubble. Bandi clawed at the rock while Stephen pulled. His side ached; his breath came in gasps as he tugged. A second tank rolled into sight.

They couldn't leave the old man. Stephen let go for a moment, hooked the end of the metal piece under a huge boulder and leaned on it with all his weight. It shifted slightly, then rolled sideways. The old man was free.

He and Bandi half-carried, half-dragged him into the safety of the Barracks. The man felt light, trembling beneath them. It was like carrying a child.

They were safe now in the cool darkness of the Barracks, the noise from outside muffled by the thick walls. Dini's uncle, medical bag in hand, waited for them.

Stephen eased the man down onto a cot, then leaned against the stone wall. His legs buckled. The room tilted; he held his head still, trying to stop the dizziness.

"You, Stephen, need some rest." He felt the doctor's hand on his shoulder, guiding him into the next room. "We've got everything under control. Sleep." Stephen lay down on the cot, but he could not sleep.

His muscles jerked with the sound of the gunfire outside. The walls of the Barracks seemed to close in on him, then fade away. Was this just the dizziness?

The light in the room changed, got brighter, then darker again. He saw his father standing in the doorway, and behind him, the White Stag. He sat up quickly, his heart pounding. No one was there.

Now he heard Mária. She was crying, calling out to him, begging him to play the piano for her, but he couldn't move. Was he asleep? He tried to force himself to wake up, to call out for help, but his voice sounded no more than buzzing in a dark hole.

Finally, what seemed a long time later, he woke, soaked with sweat, his jaw clenched and aching.

He listened.

The battle outside had stopped.

He could see nothing but shadows when he sat up and looked out the window of the Barracks. He coughed; the smell of gunfire still hung in the air.

In the quiet around him, his mind formed a single thought.

Apu. Was it possible he was still alive—one of the prisoners who had been released? Was the rumor George had heard true? The thought wouldn't leave him. He had to go home. He had to see if Apu was there.

Pali slept on a mat in the corner; he moaned now in his sleep and shifted his bandaged leg. Stephen covered him with the wool blanket that had slipped to the floor. He scrawled a note and left it on Pali's cot. Then he made his way out of the Barracks, taking one of the back exits.

A cold drizzle misted the buildings. The side streets were blocked by disabled tanks, some of them still smoking. The wet ashy smell caught in his throat.

The buildings looked like shattered toys; a roof at the corner hung crazily with only one beam to support it. Across the street a crucifix hung from a section of wall where a house had once stood. The wall itself had been split by shell fire; only the one portion remained, a curtain fluttering from the open window.

In front of him, an entire house had collapsed into the street. There was no way to get around it. He crawled up and through the rubble, trying to avoid shards of broken glass. His hand came down on something soft. He looked down.

A child's arm. His heart pounded.

No. A rag doll. Relief flooded him as he lifted it up, the pale cloth body smudged with ash.

He brushed it off, setting it on a broken chairseat, then scrabbled on through the wreckage.

Furniture lay in splinters, a piece of a cabinet here, a shattered drawer there. A dining room table lay upside down, the curved claw legs reaching up like empty arms.

A tangle of flowers lay next to it, and a blue glass vase, tipped on its side but unbroken. Stephen stared at it; he knew that vase. Ferenc's Aunt Lili used it often for the centerpiece at special dinners.

Ferenc, with whom he'd attended school from second grade on. He frowned. Could this be the aunt's house? He looked around. A small section of dining room wall poked up out of the wreckage.

That wallpaper. Tiny pink roses against a background of twisting vines. There was no doubt in his mind now; he was in Aunt Lili's house.

Where was she now? And Ferenc, and Uncle Miklós? He considered this, feeling strangely numb inside. It didn't matter. None of this seemed real anyway.

Crawling out of the wreckage, he stood. Still, nothing looked familiar.

Where was the butcher shop? The newsstand? Mrs. Széna's little dress shop, where Mária had bought her wedding dress? They should all be here, across from Ferenc's apartment building, but he saw none of them, not even a recognizable shell. Only this pile of rubble, reaching the entire block.

He reached out to steady himself. His hand touched a

metal plate—a street sign. Leaning close in the darkness, he tried to make out the letters on the sign. A shot whistled through the air. Stephen hit the ground, flattening himself behind a pile of brick and cement. He lay still, holding his breath. No more shots. The sniper had moved on.

He felt tired now, so tired he could fall asleep right on top of this pile of rock. He tried to rouse himself. He must not fall asleep here. Maybe he was not where he thought he was. Maybe this was all a dream.

For a moment, he thought he was a small boy again and had fallen. Playing soccer with Dini, he'd cut his leg. Mária had hurried to him, lifted him up, washed away the dust and blood, bandaged his scratched knee.

Mária. He had to see Mária—and Apu. He must see if Apu had escaped, had come home to him. He struggled again to read the name on the street sign, squinting his eyes to clear away the blurriness. József Boulevard.

He raised his head and looked around. He saw it now: the stone cherub protruding from the corner of the building fifty feet away. Less than a block from home.

He stumbled toward his house, making his way around jagged piles of concrete and splintered planks. Almost there, he fell and came down hard on a piece of broken cement. His whole leg felt numb for a moment, then began to ache.

Looking up, he saw the gray stone of his own apartment building.

Still standing. It seemed impossible.

The outside door was buried halfway to the top with rubble. Even if he pounded on it and the manager heard him, he wouldn't be able to get in.

If he could just climb up to the second story and reach Mária's window—someone might hear him and let him in that way. It wasn't so far to climb with this mound of stone and cement.

But it would make him a perfect target for the sniper.

For any AVO patrolling in the area.

No choice. Struggling for footholds, he inched up the side of the wall, his hands aching as he grasped the uneven brick. A shot whistled through the air just as he reached the window. The sniper again, from the building across the street. He pounded on the frame. A fragment of broken glass fell, clinking on the pile of debris below. A second shot split the air. He pulled frantically at the remaining glass in the heavy frame, breaking it away in pieces, until the window opening was clear. A trickle of blood oozed from his thumb.

Another shot; this one whizzed by his ear.

He forced his head and shoulders through the window opening. Twisting, he struggled into the room. He fell to the floor with a thump. He lay there, trying to catch his breath. Outside, all was quiet.

The sound of running footsteps in the hall, and now Mária's terrified face looked down at him. "My God. Stephen! Are you hurt?" She knelt beside him and sponged off his face with the cloth in her hand. It felt cool, so cool.

"I came up for more bandages. You scared me to death."

He looked up at her. He couldn't speak. He could barely keep his eyes open. Gently she stroked his forehead. "It's all right, Stephen, it's all right. You're safe here."

Chapter 10
The Two Battles

Sunday, October 28

When he woke, he was on a bed in the cellar. A cobweb fluttered above him, and moisture beaded the wall. He lifted his head. Mária sat a few feet away, watching him.

"Apu. Where's Apu?"

Mária's face looked pale above him. "What do you mean, Stephen?"

"The prisoners . . . George said prisoners were released."

She looked puzzled, then her face cleared. "Oh. George told me about that rumor." She gently stroked his forehead. "Stephen, even if Apu were still alive, he'd be in one of the prisons far away, outside the city."

Stephen was silent. Apu wasn't here. How could he have believed he might be? He swallowed down his disappointment. "Where is everyone?" His voice sounded loud in the cellar.

Mária put a finger to his lips. He looked over and saw a

boy sleeping on a cot behind the iron stove. "Mother's back at the Telex machine again, and Grandmother's at the apartment building on the next block. The doctor asked her to help with some wounded."

"They left you alone?"

"Dini's been here with me. He just went out a few minutes ago to get more food."

Stephen rubbed his head. "How long have I been sleeping? I don't remember coming down to the cellar."

Mária smiled. "I practically had to carry you, falling asleep at every step. It's almost six in the morning now." She laid a warm hand against his cheek. "Are you sure you're all right? You feel so cold."

He didn't want to tell her about his hallucinations or this numbness he felt inside since that day of the Massacre. "I'm . . . all right. I was worried about you."

"Stephen, you must know George was here yesterday and everything was fine. He checks on me every day." She looked at him for a long moment. "Come, I'll get you a glass of water and then some soup."

He drank the water without speaking, its coolness soothing his throat. Mária dished up a bowl of potato soup and sat down beside him. A look of pain crossed her face, and she winced.

Stephen stiffened. "Is it the baby?"

"I think the baby is just warming up. Don't be worried. Eat your soup, and then you can help me feed Janos, the boy on the cot over there. He's not badly wounded, but he's exhausted. He and two friends defended a street intersection for three nights with no one to relieve them." Tears filled Mária's eyes. "He's younger even than you, Stephen, just barely thirteen."

He said nothing.

"My poor Stephen. You have seen terrible things these past few days." Mária watched him for a moment, her eyes dark with concern. "Let's sit and talk . . . the way we used to." She leaned over and took his hand. "Remember when you and I used to go to Gellért Hill and pick the buttercups and daisies? I pretended to cry one time, because you had the best ones." She smiled. "I was only teasing, but you gave me your whole bouquet."

"I remember." He felt a stirring inside. Somewhere deep. Like ice melting.

They sat quietly for several minutes. "Remember, Stephen, the first time I brought George to the house and he carried in two chickens wrapped in brown paper? Mother made chicken *risotto,* and we had a feast. You had the most amazed look on your face. You asked George if he was rich."

"I couldn't imagine anyone having two chickens at once for a meal. It wasn't even a special holiday."

"Yes it was, though you had no way of knowing. That was the night George asked me to marry him." Mária looked dreamy. "Do you remember the kitten George brought me? That was an engagement present."

"Cirmi." Stephen remembered the little gray puffball. "She looked like Miska."

"Oh yes—our little Miska, from so long ago. I loved to play with her up in the attic on rainy days when we were little. Remember, Stephen, how she tumbled after that red ribbon when you dangled it in front of her?"

He nodded. It was hard to believe that he had once been that small boy, so carefree.

Janos, on the cot in the corner, groaned and woke up.

Mária jumped up and dished him a bowl of soup. He seemed stronger now that he had slept. He ate the soup, then decided to make his way home.

Stephen knew he should go, too, should get back to the Barracks, but he didn't want to leave Mária alone. He'd wait until Dini arrived.

Mária shifted in her chair and got up to pace before sitting down again. "Don't worry, Stephen. These cramps I'm having are normal. The baby won't come for a couple days more."

But another hour went by, and Mária stopped her attempts at conversation. He watched as she rubbed her back. She bent over and moaned.

Stephen stood up. "I'll go get Grandmother."

Mária wiped the perspiration from her forehead.

"No, Stephen, please don't. The doctor needs her. I'll be fine for a little longer. Dini will soon be back." She tried to smile. "Besides, you're here to help me."

His hands felt cold; he put them in his pockets. He had no idea how to help deliver a baby.

He heard a new sound from outside, and the ground trembled. Now, of all times, they didn't need a Soviet tank in the neighborhood. Stephen cursed under his breath.

Bullets whistled overhead. He heard explosions as the tank fired randomly at the houses in the block. The tank creaked as it turned, and a sudden blast rattled the glass front of the cabinet by the stove. Mária grabbed his arm.

Stephen swallowed down his own fear to reassure her. "We're safe here in the cellar, Mária. Come, lie down."

"No, not yet. It helps if I keep walking." She paced back and forth between the bed and the stairs. Suddenly she gave a sharp cry and doubled over, clutching her stomach.

Stephen's heart thudded. He wiped her face with a clean towel and led her to the big empty bed in the corner. What could be taking Dini so long?

His grandmother had prepared the bed before she left, covering it with clean linens. She had two stacks of fresh towels ready, and clothes for the baby wrapped in a sheet. Mária lay quietly, crying out only when one of the labor pains overwhelmed her.

Stephen walked back and forth, listening as the firing above grew louder. He went to the stove and boiled a pan of water, remembering that someone had said to do so. What for? He couldn't remember, and he didn't want to ask Mária, for fear of making her own anxiety worse.

Mária gave a little gasp, a shocked look on her face. "Stephen! The water! It's just broken." The dark stain showed through the blanket. Stephen changed the bedding, feeling clumsy. He wished now he had watched that day when Dini had helped Grandmother deliver Mrs. Kovács's baby.

Mária seemed to sense his confusion, and gave him quick instructions. "Bring the water you boiled, Stephen. We must get ready for the birth. I think it will be soon. And boil fresh water for the scissors and cotton strips to tie the cord."

He did as he was told, while sweat poured down his face. Why in God's name had Mária decided to have the baby now? Why couldn't she have waited a few days? He had no idea what to do when the baby started to come.

He slammed the fresh pan of water down on the stove and struggled with the match to relight the burner. Mária moaned, her body tightening as a new contraction hit her. He fought an urge to rush up the stairs and out to the street—to shout for someone, anyone to help.

But there was no help. Only the tank, blasting away at the buildings above him. He felt panic rising in his chest. What if he just left? Took a back route and went back to the Barracks?

It was late afternoon now. Mária's breathing came in shallow gasps; her pains seemed almost constant. She sobbed and reached for his hand, clinging to it.

This was worse than any of the battles he'd fought the last few days. His heart pounded harder now than it had yesterday when he'd run from that sniper.

Even Pali would be afraid here.

He waited until she dozed off fitfully. Then he released her fingers and started toward the stairway.

Mária opened her eyes. "Stephen, don't leave me. Where are you going?" Her voice sounded fluttery.

"I . . . I'm going to get Grandmother." A coward. He was a coward, just as Pali had told him so many times.

A contraction hit her then, a powerful one. She arched her back and fought it, her face twisting. "No! Oh, *no,* Stephen. Don't leave me!" She held out her hands, pleading.

He stumbled in his hurry to get back to her side. "Mária, Mária. Hush . . . it's all right." There was no way. No matter how afraid he felt, he couldn't leave her, not now.

How could he calm her? Barely thinking what he was doing, he began to recite the poem Apu had told him so long ago—the story of the White Stag.

"The bird flies from branch to branch
The song flies from lips to lips
Grass becomes green on the old grave . . .
The White Stag rises . . ."

His voice shook, then strengthened. He was surprised; he didn't know he remembered so many of the words. Just saying them out loud calmed him.

Mária's body relaxed, and she slumped limply into the bed. When he finished the poem, she looked up at him. "You tell it so well, Stephen. If I close my eyes, I can almost hear Apu's voice." She sighed. "It's so hard to think he will never see his grandchild."

"Don't say that!" Stephen said. "He may still be alive in one of the prisons. He may be released, even now." Mária was quiet for a few moments, seeming to doze. She woke suddenly, her face contorted in pain. The contractions came one after another now, with hardly a rest between them.

Mária seemed unaware of what was going on around her. She called out for George. She moaned and twisted, and her whole body shook with a violent chill. She called for Anyu, and for Grandmother.

Then, tears rolling down her cheeks, she whispered, "Daddy—Apu—Daddy. Oh, Daddy, I need you."

Stephen squeezed her hand. He felt small, six years old again, as if he'd just lost his father. He remembered kneeling on the bed in the darkness, trying to console Mária as she sobbed. He felt as helpless now as he did that night so long ago. If only he'd stayed at the Barracks yesterday. But then Mária would be alone.

The noise from outside grew louder. A tremendous explosion rattled the kettle and bowls on the stove. The electricity went out. Broken glass fell into the coal chute— their one window to the outside. He lit a kerosene lamp, and rushed to close the chute. Mária's eyes fluttered open. "Oh, Stephen! I just want to die."

He looked down at his sister. What could he say to her? He couldn't imagine what this pain of giving birth was like. The look on her face reminded him of the young mother's face that day in Parliament Square.

But that woman had died, and her child along with her. Mária cried out again, and he stroked her hair. "It's all right, Mária. The baby's almost here. I promise you." He didn't know. He hoped it was so. The pain on Mária's face eased for a moment, and she dropped off to sleep.

But the shooting overhead triggered terrible memories for Stephen. He was in a nightmare, a nightmare where nothing good could survive.

And a baby was trying to be born.

He prayed—prayed as he'd never prayed before, unsure even if there was a God to pray to—that Mária might live and her baby also.

The gunfire was almost directly above them now. The entire cellar was dark except for one small pool of light shed by the kerosene lamp next to Mária, who shifted restlessly in her sleep.

She woke, and he heard her low moaning as she pushed. The sound was a growl deep in her throat.

It frightened him, but he realized that she was trying to push this baby out into the world.

She opened her eyes and looked at him. "It's like falling down, down, and you don't think you will ever come up," she said. She closed her eyes, and her face turned dark as she bore down.

He spread fresh towels under her, and blood and water gushed out. Now he could see the top of the baby's head. "Stephen, oh, Stephen!" Mária's breath came in panting moans, and she gave a wrenching cry.

He waited close beside her, ready to do what he must do. But he was no longer afraid.

The baby's face appeared, the eyes closed, the nose slightly flattened. He watched, holding his breath. The little one, not yet fully born, opened his mouth and let out a weak cry.

Mária pushed again, and the baby slid into Stephen's hands.

Warm, slippery. A boy. Stephen's hands shook as he placed him on Mária's stomach. The baby squirmed and began to wail.

Mária touched the small face and body, laughing and crying at the same time. Stephen dried the baby with a clean towel, while Mária told him how to cut and tie the cord.

He did as he was told, feeling clumsy. He wrapped the baby in a soft flannel blanket and handed him to Mária.

She cupped the baby's face in her hand and traced the outline of his nose with her finger. She unwrapped the blanket and looked carefully at his small body. Gently she pried open the baby's hand and kissed it. The tiny fingers closed around her thumb.

She looked up at her brother and smiled. "We shall call him Stephen," she said.

Chapter 11
What Happened to Dini

Stephen looked down at the rumpled, blood-stained sheets, and at Mária, lying exhausted with the baby in her arms. He listened. It was quiet outside now. He could hear rain falling, washing the blood away from the streets. The battle was over.

The baby let out a wail. Mária put him to her breast, and he nursed with loud sucking sounds.

His sister looked peaceful now. "I remember when you were born, Stephen. I loved you the first moment I saw you. I thought you were a special kind of doll, just for me."

He smiled. "I thought big sisters were jealous of new babies."

"I wasn't. I would stand by your cradle, the wooden one Apu carved for you, and watch as you slept. When you cried, I'd bring you every little toy I could think of to make you smile." She looked tenderly down at her new son, then up at Stephen. "Even as a baby you loved music. When Grandmother played the piano, you'd stop whatever you were doing—playing or crying—and just listen. Apu said even then that you would grow up to be a musician." Reaching out, she touched Stephen's hand. "Someday, you will go to the Music Academy."

"I hope so." He thought of the music rooms at the Academy. Grandmother had described them to Stephen, telling him often of when she had been a student there so many years ago.

The huge concert halls, the practice rooms with gleaming pianos, kept always in perfect tune. It was hard to believe he might go there. But, if their revolution succeeded . . .

The heavy door above them opened suddenly. Stephen looked up to the top of the stairs.

"Grandmother!" Mária called out joyfully. Grandmother climbed down the steps, holding a brown paper parcel. At the sight of the baby, she stopped. "Your great-grandson," Mária said softly.

"Holy Mother of God. You've had the baby, Mária! When was he born? Are you both all right? Let me see him!" Rushing to Mária's side, Grandmother wrapped her and the baby in a trembling hug. Tears crept down her wrinkled cheeks as she traced a cross on the baby's forehead.

"He's beautiful. He looks like you, Stephen, when you were a baby. The same dark hair. And look at his long fingers; perhaps he will be a pianist, too!" Gently she tucked another blanket around Mária and the baby. "As soon as he is finished nursing, I will hold him."

She looked around. "But where is Dini? He promised he would stay with you."

"He went out for food, Grandmother, but he's been gone a long time now." Mária looked over at Stephen. "It was my brother who helped with the birth." She smiled. "I was terrified, but he stayed so calm."

Stephen swallowed. He'd come so close to deserting her. He was glad she didn't know.

Grandmother kissed him on both cheeks. "Thank God you were here, Stephen."

A shadow of worry crossed her face. "I don't understand why Dini left and hasn't returned. I counted on him to be here. I would have come back sooner, but the shelling was so heavy." She stood looking at Mária and the baby. "But now, Mária, you must eat." She walked over to the stove. "I will fix a rich chicken broth, so you will have good milk for my great-grandson." Taking out a big pot, she put vegetables to simmer on the stove. Stephen watched as she opened the brown paper parcel and held up a plump chicken, ready for cooking. "This is for the soup. The doctor sent it with me." She took out another pan, quickly cut up the chicken, and put it with onions in the pan to brown. Stephen's stomach rumbled as the chicken began to sizzle, the delicious smell filling the cellar.

His grandmother. She was always happiest cooking—her way of showing love.

The heavy door at the top of the steps crashed open. Stephen jumped to his feet, his hand on his gun.

George. His face streaked with grime and sweat, his clothes black with oil from weapons.

Bandi stumbled down the stairs after him, the two of them maneuvering a stretcher with someone on it. Stephen's hands turned cold as he saw the scratched face.

Dini. Blood soaked through a bandage wrapped around his chest.

"Quick, Stephen," George said. "Help us get him onto the cot. I found him a couple of blocks from here. He's been shot." Mária sat up on her bed in the dim far corner. But George's whole attention was on Dini, as he slid him gently onto the cot. "I don't know how bad the wound is. There was too much blood to tell. We had to bandage him quickly and get him here before more tanks arrived."

Grandmother hurried over with clean sheets and a blanket. "He'd gone out only to get food. How could this happen?"

"A tank captain fired on the bread line. Dini just happened to be there."

Anger rose in Stephen's throat, almost choking him. "The bread line! Damn them."

Dini groaned and shifted restlessly on the cot. His face twisted in pain. George handed Stephen a canvas case from the foot of the stretcher. "His medical bag. See if there's some pain medicine left."

Stephen fumbled through the contents of the bag and found the vial of medicine and a syringe. His hand shook as he handed the syringe to Grandmother. Bandi watched, his freckles muddy against his pale face. "We'd better see how bad it is," George said. He leaned over to unwrap the bandages.

Grandmother grabbed his arm. "I'll do it. You may help, but don't touch him until you have washed." She brought a basin of hot water and soap and watched as both George and Stephen scrubbed their hands.

The bloodstained gauze stuck to the wound. Stephen winced as Grandmother soaked it with clean water and peeled away the bandages. She sponged the whole area and bent to study it. "The bullet came out here, just below his shoulder. He will recover. But the wound in the chest is deep, and he must rest so that he does not develop pneumonia."

She worked with George to clean and rebandage Dini's wounds. Just as they finished, the baby, in bed with María on the far side of the room, let out a small cry.

George froze, his bloodied hands in midair. He turned slowly around. "María?"

He stared at her as she lay quietly in bed in the shadowed corner behind the stairs. "My God."

Almost in a daze he washed his hands, then walked over to her. He looked down at the baby. "My God," he said again. "When did . . ." He looked so bewildered, Stephen had to smile. Finally George seemed to realize that this was his son. He knelt down and cradled María's face in his hands. Stephen looked away. It was a holy moment, this first meeting of father, mother, and child. It should be a moment for them alone.

"Come, Stephen," Grandmother said. "Sit with Dini and sponge his face, while I stir the soup."

She took a medal, gleaming gold in the dim light, from her apron pocket and fastened it around Dini's neck. "This medal belonged to your grandfather, Stephen. It is of St. Imre, protector of Hungary's youth. Dini shall wear it for the next few days."

Dini shifted in his sleep. Stephen sat down beside him. He had to be all right. It was always Dini who kept him from getting too serious about things in school, ready with a quick joke or a piece of *bukta* when things weren't going well.

Dini who, when they were small, had squatted in the courtyard with him, the two of them in their knickers, playing marbles day after day on a small patch of bare ground.

Dini's eyes opened, and he looked at Stephen. "What . . . what happened?"

"You had an argument with a Soviet tank. You'll be all right." Stephen worked to keep his voice steady. "But it will be a few weeks before you're well enough to cook *gulyás* again for the Scout troop." Dini grinned crookedly and drifted back to sleep.

Bandi had been quiet through all this. He came over now and stood beside Stephen. "Is he going to be okay?"

Stephen nodded. "I think so."

Grandmother cut two thick pieces of dark bread and set them on the table beside steaming bowls of soup. "Stephen, come here and get some soup. You too, Bandi." She frowned at Bandi. "What would your mother say if she saw you now? It's bad enough that you're out fighting, boy that you are. At least you must eat."

Bandi grinned, then walked over to the table. "Yes, Grandmother."

Stephen finished his soup quickly, then went back to sit at Dini's side. He dozed off. He woke with a jump when he felt George's hand on his shoulder. "Thank you for helping with the birth. I won't soon forget that you were here when we needed you most."

George sat down beside him. "Today I saw your teacher, Antal Tóth. He fought alongside us against a Soviet tank."

"So he *is* in sympathy with the Revolution. I wondered why he let Pali read the Sixteen Points in the classroom. But he's a Communist—and he never spoke against the Soviets

83

in the classroom."

"He probably felt it wasn't safe. I think he's like many Communists who attended our meetings these last few months. He believes in the ideals of Communism, but not in the methods the Soviets use. At any rate, Antal Tóth is now a freedom fighter."

George sat for a moment longer, not saying anything. His face was serious. Stephen's stomach tightened. "What is it?"

"You remember I told you there were rumors about prisoners being released? Last night twenty of them joined us at the Barracks. They had been in the Markó street prison." So the rumors were true. His heart pounded in his ears. George watched him. "We have heard that prisoners from Vác have been freed also; several men who were arrested years ago showed up in Budapest late last night."

Vác. That chamber of horrors. He'd heard the stories of torture, of prisoners going mad. It was the worst of all the prisons, if the rumors were true.

"Have you heard—" Stephen's voice stuck.

George shook his head. "No one I talked to has heard of your father. He could be in any one of a number of prisons. We'll have to wait and see what happens." George rubbed his chin. "Would he know to come here if he's released?"

"This is the apartment building we lived in when he was taken. If he could recognize it with all the shelling, he would come."

"I don't like to say this, Stephen, but the truth is, many prisoners have died." George sighed. "Eight years is a long time."

The baby whimpered from across the room. George squeezed Stephen's shoulder, then walked back over to

Mária and his new son. Stephen sat silently. George was right; he must be realistic. What were the chances after these eight years, that Apu was still alive?

The soup he'd eaten churned in his stomach. Now at least there was a chance, a small one, that he might see his father again.

He hardly dared let himself hope.

Chapter 12

The Man on the Stairs

Monday, October 29

Stephen bolted upright on his cot. Anyu bent over him, her hand brushing his face. "Are you all right, Stephen? You called out in your sleep."

For a moment he couldn't remember where he was. Then he saw Grandmother dozing in her chair by the coal chute. He was in the cellar, and it was morning.

"You're back!" he whispered to Anyu. He hugged her.

"So you are an uncle," she said. "I'm so proud of you, delivering this baby with no help from Grandmother or Dini."

"Dini! Is he all right?"

His mother nodded, putting a finger to her lips. Stephen got to his feet. His legs felt stiff; his whole body ached. He saw Dini then, asleep on the cot on the other side of the room.

Mária slept in the big bed in the corner, her dark hair

spread out on the pillow, with the baby drowsing beside her. The baby let out a cry; Anyu's face softened as Mária sleepily lifted him to her breast. "Well, we've seen one miracle. For Mária to give birth safely in the midst of that terrible shelling yesterday—truly God was with us."

Anyu sliced off two thick pieces of bread and put them on a plate. "George had to go back to the Barracks during the night. He sent Bandi home to see his mother."

Stephen looked at her. "What's happening with our Revolution?"

"The shooting has stopped for now. Some of the Soviet tanks have left, but the men at Kilián Barracks are still on alert."

"Why didn't George wake me? I should be there, too."

Anyu shook her head. "He said you should stay here at least for today, to regain your strength."

"I feel better now." Stephen went to the stove and ladled out a bowl of the chicken soup.

Grandmother woke up. She leaned forward and turned on the radio. "Let us see what the Soviets are up to today."

Static crackled, then the voice of the announcer. " . . . According to Prime Minister Imre Nagy, the cease-fire is effective as of today, and Soviet troops have begun with-drawal. We repeat, Soviet troops have begun withdrawal."

Grandmother's eyes brightened. She heaved herself out of her chair and kissed Stephen on both cheeks. "I knew once Gerô was gone, Imre Nagy would be able to make the Soviets leave. Just wait. You will see! Perhaps now, they will even release the cardinal from prison."

Cardinal Mindszenty. Grandmother prayed for him every day, Stephen knew. All these years, since he'd first been imprisoned. The radio returned to its regular program. Stephen listened to the soothing strains of Beethoven's *Pastorale* Symphony. Through the coal chute, he could see a beam of light. Perhaps it was true. Perhaps today the troops would leave, and Hungary would finally be free.

The cellar door opened. A man's feet started down the stairs.

Stephen picked up his gun. Anyu held his arm. Stephen stood, tense, watching. In the dim light, he could barely make out the slender figure of the man moving slowly down the steps. A patched coat hung on his gaunt frame. His face was dark with unshaved beard.

Stephen's hand tightened on the gun. The man was almost to the bottom of the stairs now. He looked up.

Stephen's heart hammered.

Those dark eyes.

Behind him, Anyu let out a choked cry. "István!" There was the sound of metal hitting the stone floor as Grandmother dropped the soup ladle.

"Apu?" Stephen mouthed the word, but no sound came out.

"Stephen," his father whispered. "My son."

The world suddenly tilted. Stephen stumbled the last few steps to his father.

In the background, the baby wailed as Mária bolted up in the old iron bed. For Stephen, it all seemed dim and far away.

He felt the rough tweed of Apu's coat against his face and the wetness of tears running down his cheeks.

For now, he was a little boy again, six years old, safe in his father's arms.

Chapter 13
The White Stag

Anyu's voice cried out over and over, "István, my dear one." Grandmother and Anyu clung to Apu along with Stephen, each trying to hold, to touch some part of him. And then from the corner, Mária, palefaced, tried to get up from her bed. "Daddy, Apu. Oh, Daddy. It *is* you!"

"Mária!" Anyu took a warning step forward. "You can't get up. It's too soon. We will come to you." Anyu clung to Apu, supporting him as he limped over to the big bed where Mária lay.

Apu bent over her. "*Édeském, édes kislányom*—My sweet one, my sweet little girl." He knelt down beside Mária and touched her hair.

He saw the baby then. For a moment no one moved, no one spoke.

Mária wrapped the baby in his blanket and held him up to her father. "Apu, this is your new grandson. Would you like to hold him?" And then his father did cry, sitting on the bed beside Mária, his shoulders shaking. Stephen,

Grandmother, and Anyu stood beside him in a protective circle, their arms around him, until finally his tears stopped.

He looked around the cellar almost fearfully as he held his grandchild.

"It's all right," Anyu said, laying her hand gently on his arm. Apu's stiff shoulders relaxed, and he sat for several moments, cradling the baby, staring into the sleeping face. Finally he looked up at them, standing around him. "I am home," he said. "I am really home."

Grandmother walked heavily over to the stove. "And now, István, you must eat. You are so thin." Stephen watched her dish up a bowl of the thick chicken soup. His grandmother, always urging them to eat.

The ghost of a smile touched his father's lips. "Yes, my Mamushka." He kissed the baby and handed him back to Mária. Then, leaning on Stephen, he shuffled to the table and sat down.

His father's hand shook as he lifted the first spoonful of soup to his mouth. How long had it been since he had eaten? He ate slowly, turning his head, looking around the cellar. He was frightened, even now, even here with his family. What had the AVO done to him to make him this afraid? A truck rolled by in the street above, sending a few pieces of coal clattering down the chute. Apu jumped, and dropped his spoon. He sat stiffly, ready to defend himself. Again Anyu touched his arm. "It is all right, István. You are safe here."

His father closed his eyes for a moment, then opened them. "It is so hard to believe . . . that I am no longer in prison."

Anyu put her arm around him and pulled him close, like

a small child. "So many times, my István, I thought of that last day we spent together in the country, before you were taken away."

Apu looked at Stephen. "When I left, you came barely to my knee." He hesitated. Now . . . you are as tall as me."

Anyu laughed, a choked laugh, almost a cry. "He's fourteen now, István."

Stephen's throat ached. All those years, his father had been gone. "Apu." He swallowed, then went on. "Which prison?"

His father's face looked gray, and once more he turned to look around the room. His chest rose and fell, just once. "Vác. I was at Vác."

Stephen shivered.

No wonder his father was so afraid.

Anyu took his trembling hand in both of hers. He looked at her. "Eight years of darkness . . ." He closed his eyes for a moment, and a look of pain crossed his face.

"I hate them," Stephen muttered. "I hate them for doing this to you!"

His father looked up. "No, Stephen. You must not hate. Hate destroys." He took a deep breath. "All those years at Vác, I held fast . . . to my memories of you. It is how I survived." Apu's head went down, his chin resting on his chest, as if the weight of remembering was too heavy. Finally he looked up.

"That last night, Stephen, while you slept, I . . . carved something." He reached for his tattered jacket, hanging on the chair beside him, and handed it to Stephen. "Look in the pocket."

Stephen felt inside the ragged pocket.

"Deeper," Apu said. "Reach into the lining."

He felt it then, the bit of wood, intricately carved. Stephen pulled the small figure from Apu's jacket pocket.

The White Stag.

Small, less than two inches, but perfectly formed, carved from white pine.

Apu's voice was a whisper. "I carried it . . . in my pocket that night. In all these eight years . . . I have managed to hold on to it. And it has reminded me of all of you, of our times together."

"István, you must rest," Anyu said.

He held up his hand. "Soon. There is more . . . I must tell you." He looked around at each of them, at Anyu, Stephen, Grandmother, and over to Mária, sitting up in bed with the baby, watching her father with shining eyes.

"My hope was no bigger . . . than that bit of wood." Apu gestured weakly toward the stag in Stephen's hand. "But I held fast to my small hope. Each day I would repeat to myself your names, my memories of each of you." His voice faded to a whisper. "I knew somehow . . . God would lead me home to you." He closed his eyes then, and leaned back against Anyu.

"Now, István," she said. "Now rest."

When his father woke, Grandmother insisted he eat more soup. He ate slowly, but his hand no longer trembled. When he finished, he carefully wiped the inside of the bowl with a folded bit of bread.

Stephen smiled. He remembered this. When he was a small boy, Apu did this same thing.

"Did the freedom fighters rescue you?" Grandmother asked. "Come, István, tell us."

Apu shook his head. "One of our own prisoners." He sat silently for a moment, remembering. "Do you know how Vác is? The waves of the Danube River lap . . . against one wall of it." He was quiet, gathering strength to go on. "Last week we heard a shout from that side . . . telling us we would be free."

"Someone in a boat," Stephen said.

Apu nodded. "Probably a rowboat passing by. From that moment . . . things changed."

"What things?" Anyu asked gently.

"The guards . . . hid their uniforms. Put on civilian clothes." Apu drew in a deep breath.

"There's a patch of sky, above street level. That afternoon . . . we saw our flag, with the red star torn out." Apu leaned forward, his voice strengthening. "From cell to cell prisoners began to shout. The guards threatened . . . but it did them no good. We were no longer afraid."

"But who released you, István? Was it the guards?" Grandmother asked.

Apu shook his head. "A man . . . in the next cell. Somehow he . . . got hold of a revolver. Shot off the lock. A thousand of us escaped." He put his arm around Stephen's shoulder and let out a long sigh. "I am home. I am really home. I thank God for each of you."

"And we, for you." Grandmother patted Apu's shoulder. "Did you have a hard time finding the house, my son?"

He nodded. "Even when I started down the stairs, I wasn't sure I had the right house."

He seemed drained now, and leaned back in the chair, his arm slipping from Stephen's shoulder. It was hard to see his once strong father so weak, so exhausted.

The radio crackled in the corner. Grandmother stood up and moved closer. "The music has stopped. They are going to make another announcement! Perhaps it will be about the cardinal."

Apu opened his eyes. "The cardinal . . . a good man. He, too, knows . . . what it means to be tortured for what you believe."

Grandmother nodded. "There is no one holier, no one more faithful to his people than the cardinal."

A voice boomed through the static. "This is Radio Kossuth reporting. The Minister of the Interior has abolished the AVO. There will be no need for such an organization in our democratic public life."

Grandmother banged the table delightedly with the soup spoon. "No more AVO!" she said. "Now we can begin to experience some of this freedom we have gained."

"Thank God," Apu whispered. "The devil himself could cause no more trouble than the security police."

Stephen thought suddenly of Jóska and his AVO father. What would happen to them now?

Chapter 14

What Happened to Jóska's Father

Tuesday, October 30

The Soviets were moving out. Finally.

Stephen stood beside Pali and watched as two tanks lumbered along Rákóczi Street toward the outskirts of town. Several trucks followed. Each pulled a field kitchen with a bright fire glowing below and steam puffing from the chimney.

"We're free, Pali. Free. I can't believe it. And my father . . . " His throat tightened. It still felt like a dream that Apu was back. "We stayed up last night, talking."

Pali looked at him. "How is he?"

"Weak. And afraid. He stiffens at every sound. But I think his mind is sound."

"Be thankful, then. One of Maléter's aides found old János Lasky wandering the street yesterday—released from

Vác as well. He muttered and made no sense. His mind is gone."

"Apu will recover. I can feel it. Deep inside, his spirit is still alive. And no matter what happens, I'll never let them take him away again."

"Your father's safe. Little Hungary has forced the Soviets to leave." Pali took a deep breath of the cold air. "Finally we taste freedom. I like it."

Stephen picked his way along József Boulevard, slowing his pace so Pali, still limping from his episode at Café Hungaria, could keep up.

"Stephen, I've sometimes thought you were a coward," Pali said. "But now I see you are brave."

Stephen kicked a broken chunk of cement aside with his foot, remembering his terror in the cellar with Mária as she gave birth. He had come so close to deserting her, to leaving her alone in that moment. "You're the brave one, not me. I freeze inside when faced with danger."

"Still, you do what's needed. That's real courage. That day at the Café Hungaria, you leapt out that store window to save me even though you had reached safety." Pali thought for a moment. "Actually, that was foolish—but I'm glad you were foolish." Stephen stepped over a paving stone blocking the sidewalk. Perhaps he was not a coward after all, despite his many fears. If Pali thought he was brave . . .

They crossed the street to avoid a pile of rocks and concrete where several houses had collapsed. A young boy, chasing his friends, ran into Stephen. He caught the boy by the arm and propelled him in the other direction. "Sorry!" the boy shouted as he ran off.

Several women stood in a group on the corner, chatting

with one another. "Look at this," Stephen said. "Everyone's out today."

Pali nodded. "How long has it been since we could do this and feel safe? Even God seems to be cooperating with Hungary today; we have sunshine."

But then Stephen saw an old man and woman trudging down the street. They stopped beside a pile of debris, lifted the flag covering a body that lay next to it, then replaced the flag, walking on with their heads down.

"Looking for their son," Pali said. "Or daughter." A muscle in his cheek twitched. "Too many have died. But this time we'll hang on to our freedom."

Bodies of women and children, loaded into trucks like stacks of wood by Soviet soldiers. The image haunted Stephen. "Pali. Do you think sometimes . . . about that day at Parliament Square?"

Pali was silent for a moment, then nodded.

Was it just a week ago that it had happened? Stephen would never forget what he'd seen.

He wouldn't think of it now. He turned resolutely to watch a group of children playing. Bandi waved at them from the corner and started across the street, dodging as a young boy made a dive for something glinting in the wreckage. The boy held it up so Bandi could see. "Bullet," he said. "The American journalists will trade it for chocolate."

"I've got more if you want them." Bandi handed several cartridges to the squealing children. He looked at Stephen and Pali and reddened. "I was saving these. Besides, I like chocolate, too."

Just ahead on the right were the local Party headquarters. Stephen slowed as they reached the deserted building, running his fingers over bullet holes. He looked at the buckling wall. "The tanks really blasted this."

"Good!" Pali muttered. "That's where that group of AVO men holed up. Traitors! The best thing Nagy has done so far is to abolish the Security Police."

Bandi peered into a window of the building. "I heard yesterday some of the AVO officers were tortured and hanged."

"They deserve it," Pali said.

Stephen gave him a quick look. "Don't say it, Pali. No one should die that way."

They turned down the side street toward home. "Do you hear someone crying?" Bandi asked.

The muffled sobs were close by. Stephen hesitated, then walked up to the bombed-out building and peered through the doorway. A man's body swung from a beam in the courtyard, an AVO uniform hanging in shreds from the decaying corpse. Slumped against the wall, shoulders trembling, was a boy about his own age.

Jóska Káldor.

Stephen knew it, even before the boy looked up. Jóska, who'd betrayed them so many times in the classroom. His face was puffy, his dark hair tangled.

Stephen looked from Jóska to the decaying corpse, and back. For a moment nobody spoke. Finally Stephen choked out the words. "Jóska, it isn't . . . your father?" Jóska stared down at the ground. Stephen swallowed to control the retching in his throat.

He put his arm around Jóska's shoulder and led him away from the body, over by Bandi. Bandi's face was white. He shouldn't see this. No twelve-year-old should have to see this.

"I'll look for some boards to carry—the body on," Bandi said. He hurried to a pile of broken concrete and wooden planks. Moments later Stephen heard him vomit.

Even Pali seemed shaken as he struggled to cut down the body. When Bandi returned, dragging a wide, splintery board, Pali lifted the corpse onto it without speaking. Stephen held his breath, unable to bear the smell of the decaying body. He picked up the front end of the plank, and Pali took the back.

Jóska still hadn't spoken. He sat on the ground, staring at the swinging rope that had been his father's gallows. Stephen looked away. There was nothing they could say or do to make this better.

Bandi held out his hand and pulled Jóska to his feet. He started back toward the apartment building, pulling Jóska along with him. Stephen and Pali followed, struggling with the splintery plank, and the uneven weight of Jóska's father's body.

They had reached József Boulevard now; people looked away and moved to the other side of the street when they saw them. Stephen kept walking, his eyes straight ahead. Jóska, supported by Bandi, stumbled along with his head down.

They were almost to the apartment building when Jóska began to talk, his voice hoarse. "I never . . . found my father after I left the classroom that day. I heard rumors . . . but I couldn't find him. Today . . . some people were talking about revenge on the AVO for the death of their daughter. They said something about shooting at the headquarters, so I came here."

Jóska talked faster now, as if he couldn't stop now that

he'd started. "It was deserted. I only turned on this side street to go back to the apartment. When I turned the corner—"

Stop, Stephen wanted to say. Don't say any more.

Jóska's voice made a croaking noise. "I didn't know it was him at first. But then I saw the ring on his hand. It's the one Mother gave him before she died."

How strange to think that Jóska's mother had given his father a ring. That she could love an AVO officer, just as Anyu loved Apu. Stephen's stomach hurt.

And what about Jóska? Had his AVO father played with him when he was a baby, tossing him up, tickling him? Had he told stories to Jóska as Apu did for Stephen? Held him when he cried?

The only sound now was Pali's uneven breathing as the two of them struggled with the plank. They were almost to the apartment building.

Apu came out to meet them. He stood motionless, staring down at the shreds of uniform on the body. Terror flashed across his father's face. That AVO uniform, even in tatters—what memories must it hold for his father? Stephen felt sick, remembering the stories of torture at Vác.

Then Apu looked into Stephen's eyes. He took a deep, shaky breath and reached out to pull Jóska into his arms. Jóska sobbed, his whole body trembling, as he clung to Apu. Pali and Stephen set the plank down on the ground.

"I'll take Jóska inside," Stephen said.

His father nodded. "Anyu . . . will fix him some soup. Sit for a few minutes."

Stephen knew what his father planned to do while Jóska was in the house. As he led Jóska inside, he saw Apu leading Bandi and Pali to a pile of wood across the street from the apartment. Weak as he was, he would supervise the building of Jóska's father's casket.

Pali was scowling, his hands shoved into his pockets. Angry. Wondering, probably, how Apu could build a coffin for an officer in the AVO, this enemy who had tortured him. But Stephen understood. In broken words last night Apu had told them.

His father had refused to hate. He had held fast to his memories of love, of his family. It was how he had survived, why his mind was not broken like János Lasky and so many of the other prisoners from Vác.

The rough coffin was ready in an hour. They put the body into it. As Apu lifted the lid to nail it on, Jóska clung to the coffin, his face white. Stephen's mother put her arms around his shoulders and gently pulled him back. She held him then, cradled him as she'd cradled Stephen eight years ago when the AVO marched his father away into the night.

But Apu was here now, alive. Jóska's father was dead.

There were two bodies to be buried. The second was a freedom fighter found on Rákóczi Avenue by one of their neighbors. Stephen and Bandi carried Jóska's father's coffin, while Pali and the neighbor carried the other.

Anyu and Apu walked beside Jóska, their arms supporting him as they trudged the short distance to the park that served now as a cemetery.

Stephen and Pali dug two graves, then lowered the makeshift coffins into them. "May they rest in peace," Apu whispered. The boys shoveled earth on top of the coffins. Stephen watched as the mud from above buried both— freedom fighter and AVO officer—in a common grave.

Chapter 15

The Mystery of the Soviet Tanks

Wednesday, October 31
to Saturday, November 3

Stephen and Pali spent hours on the streets those next few days, searching for bodies. The cemeteries were full, and they had to bury the bodies quickly to avoid the danger of a typhoid epidemic. At least twice a day they walked to the little park, and each time they carried the coffin of another freedom fighter.

Wednesday, on their way back to the house, they saw a newsboy holding up a stack of papers. He shouted out the headline. "British and French Ignore UN Warning—Bomb Suez Canal!"

"Trouble," Pali muttered. "Why the hell did they have to do that now? What if the Soviets decide to ignore the UN too?"

They met George out front and told him. He shook his

head. "I pray the Soviets don't take advantage of this. With the world's attention on Suez instead of Hungary, we'd better hope the Soviets don't change their minds about giving us our freedom."

Despite the Suez news, Budapest was in a mood of celebration. Each step toward freedom was welcomed by shouted announcements and cheering in the streets: "Imre Nagy has abolished the one-party system. We'll have a choice in our elections!" And early the next day: "Placement at the university will be by ability, not on the basis of Party membership."

Finally! Now Stephen would have his chance at the Music Academy. Grandmother would be so proud if he were accepted. He was good enough to get in; he knew that deep inside. Just thinking about it made his fingers itch.

He climbed upstairs to their apartment. It was too cold to stay long with the windows broken, but he sat down at the piano and tentatively touched the keys.

Still in tune, after all the shelling. The beginnings of a musical piece stirred in his head. It had begun to move inside him that afternoon on St. Endre Island as he'd listened to the bird in the tree above him. The *Freedom* Overture, he would call it. The notes of the first movement raced through his mind, and he began to play. The melody started in the basses, moving up through the cellos and violas.

No. Too static, too pompous. Somehow, he wanted to show the depth of what had happened here in Hungary these last few days.

The White Stag!

He could see it in his mind, that mystical animal leading the Magyars on to freedom. He paused, then his fingers moved over the keys again. The majestic White Stag in its dark and mysterious dwelling place. A sinuous melody on bassoon and cello over a dark ostinato in the basses.

The long journey from the cold, high mountains to the fertile and abundant valleys. His fingers moved over the keys, hinting at the theme as the stag left the deserted shore of the salty sea, traveling on through the dangerous and misty swamps.

The single lonely notes of the piano took on the full rounded tones of each instrument in his mind. The chill air from outside the broken windows faded away; he was warm and alive now, lost in the intensity of his composition.

Trumpets. A shout of trumpets, as the White Stag made his final triumphant leap to the shore, to the land of the blue river. To Hungary, to freedom.

"There you are, Stephen."

He jumped, startled. His mother stood at the door of the apartment, and he saw by the dim light that it was almost dusk. How many hours had he been sitting here? He stood up, feeling the numbness in his fingers, suddenly realizing how cold he was. But inside, he was warm.

"I've done it, Anyu. I've composed an Overture—The *Freedom* Overture."

She hugged him. "That's wonderful, Stephen. And just in time, too; Cardinal Mindszenty has been freed. Grandmother is ecstatic! We just heard it on the radio." Tears of joy ran down his mother's face.

The next few days the weather warmed up a bit, and the family moved back up from the cellar to the comfort of their apartment. On Saturday the whole family, along with Pali, gathered around the radio to hear the cardinal's first speech after his years of imprisonment. Jóska came in to listen with them, but Stephen could see he was puzzled. "What's so important about the cardinal?" he asked.

How could they explain this to Jóska, who had not grown up in any faith?

Grandmother's face glowed. "Cardinal Mindszenty has always stood up for the rights of the people, even though he suffered terribly for it."

Jóska still looked confused.

Pali glared at him. "He's been in prison for the last eight years. The cardinal can't remember his trial—the AVO treated him with drugs and tortured him."

Jóska looked down. Anyu put her arm around his shoulder.

At that moment, the cardinal's voice filled the room. ". . . We are not enemies of anyone. We desire to live in friendship with every people and with every country."

Pali shifted restlessly. "How can he say that after all the Soviets and the AVO have done to us?" he muttered.

Stephen looked at his mother, her arm around Jóska. The cardinal was right. Hungary was free now. They would have to be willing to forgive.

But the sudden memory of a young mother falling to the ground with her baby flashed through his mind. Anger flooded him, just as it had that day at Parliament Square.

Could he ever forgive what had happened there?

The cardinal's voice continued. "Our entire position is decided by what the Russian Empire intends to do about the military force standing within our frontiers. Radio announcements say this military force is growing . . . "

Stephen's hands felt cold. His father frowned. "That

doesn't make sense. What can the cardinal mean?"

"He has only been out of prison three days," Grandmother said. "Who knows what tales the guards have told him!" She folded her arms across her apron. "Imre Nagy says the Russian troops are withdrawing. That's good enough for me. Besides, we've seen them leave Budapest with our own eyes."

But George was quiet, and Stephen tried to ignore the knot of fear in his stomach. He went outside for a walk. Newspapers were for sale on every corner; he bought two. Freedom of the press! How long it had been since Hungary had experienced that.

Pali, still limping slightly, caught up to Stephen at the corner. "Remember, we're on duty today."

Stephen sighed. They'd volunteered to bring another group of wounded back to the university hospital. "I wish we could get out of it. I've seen enough of this suffering to last me a long time."

"I agree."

The two of them took the borrowed truck and headed first out Kerepesi Avenue, past the police barracks. They'd been told the body of a freedom fighter was lying in the street near the Industrial District. They found the man beside the road near the soap factory. Someone had placed a bouquet of flowers next to the corpse, and a small candle burned in a glass container at the man's feet. Silently Stephen and Pali lifted the body into the truck.

By midafternoon, Stephen was exhausted. As they turned down Üllôi Street, after transporting two loads of patients to the hospital, a peasant flagged them down. "I have milk from the farm. Where will it be of most use?"

Pali whistled when he saw the two big cans of milk in the back of the farmer's wagon. "Follow us," Stephen said. They wove their way slowly to the hospital with the farm wagon right behind. When they arrived, Pali and Stephen led the way in, awkwardly carrying the first can of milk between them. The farmer followed with a second. A young boy with a bandaged head looked up and smiled.

"Thank God!" a nurse said when she saw them. "Their stomachs can't handle what little food we've had available." She scurried to bring mugs. Several of the patients drank three cupfuls of milk each. The nurse looked at the farmer gratefully. "It's the first time in days some of them have eaten." The old man stood in the doorway, shuffling his feet and looking pleased.

Stephen glanced at the clock on the hospital wall. "Pali, I promised Apu I'd be back in time to help with a coffin. He insists on doing it, though he's not strong enough yet. I'll ride back with this farmer if you think you can finish here."

Pali nodded. "Only one more trip, then I'll take the truck back. My mother is baking bread today, and she's promised to fry the leftover dough for *lángos*." He smiled one of his rare smiles. "I plan to be on time for that!"

Stephen rode with the farmer back toward the apartment building. They wound their way around piles of rubble still in the streets. The farmer maneuvered his horse past broken glass, hanging wires, and a tipped-over tram. As they headed down Üllôi Avenue, they passed two burned-out tanks. "Something troubles me," the farmer said to Stephen. "We are told on the radio that the Russians are leaving, but there are Soviet tanks parked on the road by our village."

"Maybe they're just giving the soldiers a chance to rest

before moving on."

The farmer shook his head. "Some of them came from the direction of Budapest, but they've been in the same place now these past two days. And more are joining them from the east."

The back of Stephen's throat felt dry. "There must be some mistake. Why would they have pulled out of Budapest if they didn't plan to leave the country? Perhaps they're staying to help with evacuation of Russian citizens here in Hungary." But even to Stephen this didn't make sense. He and the farmer were silent for the last few blocks.

When he reached home, Apu was waiting for him. As they worked together on the coffin, Stephen said nothing about his conversation with the farmer. Why should he worry Apu? He knew nothing for sure.

Dinner that night was *gulyás,* usually one of Stephen's favorite meals, but tonight he wasn't hungry. Anyu felt his forehead. "Stephen, you're doing too much. I hope you haven't picked up an illness with your trips to the hospital."

"I'm all right!" he snapped. He pushed back from the table and walked into the other room.

Mária had just finished nursing the baby. She held him up. "Look, Stephen. Your nephew wants you to hold him." The baby gazed at him intently; his lips curved into a smile. Stephen took him in his arms. The baby's fingers curled around Stephen's thumb.

So trusting. There could be tanks all around Budapest, and still this little one would smile and hold tightly to his finger. Stephen held the baby a moment longer, then handed him to Mária. He went into his bedroom, where he lay awake for a long time.

Chapter 16
The Last Battle

Sunday, November 4

Cannons!

The low BOOM!BOOM!BOOM! interrupted Stephen's dream. He sat straight up in bed.

Heavy artillery, and it was close. Stumbling out of bed, he kicked at the comforter as it tangled around his feet. He tore into his parent's room. The radio was on. Apu sat beside it, tears running down his cheeks. The Hungarian anthem was playing. As soon as Stephen heard the solemn music, he knew what had happened. The farmer had been right.

Anyu came over to him and held him tightly. "The Soviet tanks are back. Our hard-earned freedom lasted four days."

He pulled away from her. "We won't give up this easily!" He started for the door.

Apu's hand grasped his shoulder. "Wait, Stephen. Imre Nagy is about to repeat his announcement."

Taking a deep breath, Stephen forced himself to wait as

the familiar voice came over the radio. "Attention! Attention! This is Prime Minister Imre Nagy speaking. Today at daybreak Soviet troops attacked our capital with the obvious intent of overthrowing the legal democratic Hungarian government. Our troops are in combat. The government is in its place. This is my message to the Hungarian people and to the whole world."

Stephen's knuckles went white. Back in his room, he hurriedly fastened his pants and tied hand grenades onto his belt. When he came back out, Apu stood in the kitchen doorway, watching him. "Go if you must, Stephen, but . . ." His voice faded, and he stood silently.

He still looked so frail. Anyu walked over and put her arm around him. "Our only hope now is the UN. We can't survive without their help."

George and Mária came into the kitchen; the baby started to wail. Mária's hands shook as she tried to comfort him. George looked grim. "Oil is more important to them than people! It's just as I feared: the French and the British ignored the UN's decision about Suez; now the Soviets have all the excuse they need to do the same with us."

"We stopped the Soviets once before, and we'll stop them again. We can't sit around and wait for the UN to decide what to do!" Stephen hurried into the other room and got the two remaining Molotov cocktails, sticking one in each coat pocket. He picked up his submachine gun. "Are you coming, George?"

George sighed. He bent over the baby and kissed him, then held Mária for a moment. She bit her lip as tears welled up in her eyes. "Go, George. For your son's sake."

Apu stood by the door, a vacant look in his eyes.

Stephen's resolve hardened. Apu could not survive another imprisonment.

"I'll be here . . . when you get back," Apu said, as if reading Stephen's thoughts. He reached out to hug him. "There are few things worth fighting for . . . but freedom is one of them. If I were strong enough, I would fight, too."

Anyu traced a cross on Stephen's and George's foreheads. "Go, with God's blessing." Stephen turned to look back as he and George started down the street. Apu looked so thin, so weak; but his arm was around Anyu, and she leaned into him as they stood silently by the door.

At the corner they ran into Pali and Bandi, coming out from the other door of the apartment building. "Imre Nagy just appealed on the radio for Pál Maléter to return at once to his command. You know what that means." Pali looked furious. "The Soviets took him last night to their Army Headquarters, to make final arrangements about Soviet evacuation. You can bet they've kidnapped him. Murderers!" Pali strode ahead of Stephen and George down József Boulevard. "We should have known better than to trust their word."

Bandi hurried to keep up. "Maléter's aide has taken over at Kilián Barracks. He says for us to stop the tanks any way we can."

The rumbling thunder from the east was louder now. "T-54 tanks," Stephen said. "The big ones. The Soviets mean business." His mind raced. How could they possibly stop these tanks?

His next thought startled him, and he almost laughed. "Remember the industrial warehouse at the edge of our district?"

Pali looked back at him. "What of it, Stephen? We haven't time for guessing games."

"Where we were yesterday. They have liquid soap—barrels of it. We can slow down the tanks."

George stared at him for a moment, and then grinned. "It just might work. We're about ten minutes away from there. Let's go." Stephen rushed to catch up as George and Pali raced toward Kerepesi Avenue. Bandi pounded along behind. The gunfire was louder now, explosion after explosion, as the tanks fired. In the distance Stephen saw the flicker of orange and red in the sky, as buildings burned.

He was breathing hard by the time they reached the warehouse. George explained their plan to the frightened guard, and the man's frown turned to a smile. He stood aside to let them in. The building echoed with their footsteps as they hurried to the row of barrels.

Stephen struggled with a heavy keg of liquid soap as he maneuvered it out to the main road. He heard Pali cursing softly as he wrestled another barrel out behind him.

In the faint light of dawn Stephen saw the shadows of the tanks, barely distinguishable on the horizon, moving closer. "Hurry! Open the taps." He rolled his barrel into position at the edge of the road. His hands numb with cold, he fumbled with the faucet. A thick stream of liquid soap gushed out.

Pali rolled his barrel to the opposite side of the road while George and Bandi struggled with a third. Minutes later the asphalt glistened with the slippery soap.

Stephen led the way down the slope. He crouched behind the shelter of a half-collapsed building next to the warehouse. Behind him, Bandi breathed hard. Pali and

George were silent, watching.

The first tank appeared, its main gun blazing in the half-light of dawn as it launched volley after volley at the surrounding buildings.

Stephen held his breath as the tank rumbled closer, hesitated, then slipped slowly to the side of the road. The hatch on the tank went up, and he saw the tank commander's head emerge.

Muffled curses. Head back down, hatch shut, the commander tried again to move the tank forward. Again it slipped, this time sliding off the road entirely.

Pali tugged on Stephen's sleeve. "I'd love to watch, but we'd better move on."

Stephen nodded, and George called back to the guard, "Go! If you're questioned, tell them we forced you to leave." They scrambled out the back way behind the ruins.

"The soap will slow them down here, but they'll be coming in on all the main roads," Pali said. "Let's see what we can put in their way."

"I'd better check in at the Barracks. I'll try to rejoin you soon," George said. "Keep to the side streets. Then you'll have more opportunity to hide if you encounter a tank before you expect to."

Stephen saw the worried look on his face. "Go, George. They'll need you to organize the forays. Don't worry; we'll be fine."

George headed back toward the Barracks.

"Let's get over a couple of streets and work our way toward the edge of town," Pali said.

Fifteen minutes later, they came to a group of residents by an apartment house doorway. A plump young woman hurried over to them. "The Soviets will soon be here. Mr. Miskolci just came in from the country with food; he passed a line of tanks headed this way. We're going down to our cellars, and we advise you to do the same." She pulled her shawl around her shoulders and followed the others down the stairs of the building.

"So the tanks are headed this way. And we have no soap this time." Pali took a Molotov cocktail out of his pocket. He searched through a pile of rubble next to the building, then triumphantly held up a long piece of rope. "I've got an idea. Stephen, give me that Molotov cocktail from your belt. Do you have another in your pocket?"

Stephen took it out reluctantly.

"Help me tie these on. Bandi, find someplace to hide across the road. I'm going to need your signals."

"Be careful, Pali." Bandi looked worried.

"I heard some boys did this a few days ago near Széna Square." Pali positioned the three Molotov cocktails toward the center of the line, then strung it across the road, with the bombs resting in the middle.

Stephen felt an uneasy prickling on the back of his neck. "I don't like this, Pali."

"It works. The treads suck up the bottles, then we wrap paper around a rock, light it, and throw it to explode the gasoline bombs."

Once Pali had something in mind, it was useless to try to stop him. Stephen crossed the road to stand with Bandi. Pali pulled newspaper out of the rubble and fumbled in his jacket pocket for matches.

It wasn't long before Stephen heard the echoing booms of the first tank. It made its way down the road, mounted turret gun blasting. One after the other, walls collapsed. Stephen stood, stunned, as each one crumbled to a pile of rocks and dust. Senseless. This was senseless.

The tank was a dozen yards away. Pali adjusted the rope until the gasoline bottles were positioned in line with the huge tank treads. From across the road, Bandi signaled Pali that his lineup was true.

The tank moved slowly toward the unseen rope. Closer . . . closer . . .

The tank veered slightly to the left, the monstrous treads just missing the three bottles.

Damn. Stephen wanted to rush out and throw himself against this tank—to somehow stop it. He understood Pali's fury now. The tank slowed.

Stephen tensed, grabbed Bandi's arm. "He's figured it out. Behind the building—fast."

He stood up, signaled Pali, and pointed at the building behind him.

Pali shook his head, fumbled with the hand grenade on his belt. Stephen could almost hear his muffled curse.

"Don't do it, Pali. Don't do it!" He heard his own voice, a hoarse whisper that Pali couldn't possibly hear.

Pali was in the street now, running. He threw the grenade. It rose in a slow arc, heading toward the tank. Pali turned to run for cover.

Stephen saw everything superimposed then, three images he would never forget.

The hatch of the tank swung open. There was a flash of red light and the sharp crack of rifle fire.

The tank began to burn and the ammunition inside exploded, shaking the ground beneath them.

And in that sudden glow, Pali fell, a shadow against the flickering orange and red flames.

Stephen heard a scream. His own voice, he realized with surprise.

Pali lay bleeding by the side of the road.

Then Stephen was running—running to save Pali once again. He bent down, grasped Pali under his shoulders. Heavy. He was so heavy. Stephen's hands felt warm, sticky against Pali's shirt as he pulled. "Come on, Pali," he muttered. "Just a few more feet." His words rang in his head, over the roar in his ears.

He dragged Pali's sagging body over the broken stone wall. He kicked at the rubble, cleared a spot, laid Pali down. Kneeling beside him, he listened for Pali's breath. There was none. Pali lay crumpled beside the pile of concrete and broken rock, his eyes glassy, staring up at the sky. From somewhere behind him, Bandi was shouting.

What was he saying?

Stephen heard only that dull roar in his ears.

Then, a sudden soft feeling in his side, a single sharp pain like a knife piercing, and everything went black.

Chapter 17
Red Flowers and Pain

He was in a dark hole. No, a tunnel, with no way out. Red flowers everywhere, but they kept bursting and turning into pools of blood. He was floating, floating on red waves . . .

And now he was cold, and aching everywhere, and there was a terrible pain in his right side. He tried to open his eyes, but they seemed glued shut.

He moved his head slightly and tried again. This time he saw Bandi's face above him, white, his freckles standing out in pale blotches.

"Stephen!"

The ground shook with a tremendous explosion, and Bandi threw himself down beside him. "Stephen, you have to move! This wall is going down fast!"

"Where's Pali?" His voice came out in a hoarse whisper, and he knew the answer before he asked.

"He's dead, Stephen. We'll have to carry him back. Can you walk?"

He didn't answer. Pali was dead. Pali, his friend—the one

who always knew what to do, who always won.

Until this time.

Stephen pulled himself to a sitting position, wincing as pain seared through his side. Bandi had hoisted Pali's body over his shoulder and was struggling to stand up. "Stephen, hurry! The soldiers are furious. The front tank's on fire, blocking the road."

Stephen stared as Pali's hand hung limply, bouncing against Bandi's shoulder. He felt numb now and cold all over. Pali was dead. Stephen fought a wave of pain and nausea—enemies that threatened to overwhelm him. He would not give in to them. Pali would not have given in.

"Bandi . . . leave him. I need . . . help. Come back . . . later." Each word, each breath was a knife cutting into Stephen's side. He struggled to his feet, using a wooden post from the debris to pull himself up. Everything started to go black.

There they were, the red flowers again. Through them he saw Bandi moving toward him, a hazy blur. He leaned on Bandi's shoulder. After a few minutes his head cleared. "Over there, Bandi." His mouth was fuzzy, dry—his words a whisper. He concentrated on what he had to say, pointed to the archway, still standing though the rest of the building had crumbled. "The stairs. Get help."

Another blast. Instinctively, Stephen threw himself down. He gasped with pain and bit his lip to keep from screaming out, tasting the saltiness of his own blood.

Less than half of the remaining wall was still standing. "Hurry, Bandi." Stephen struggled to his feet once more as Bandi pushed aside a pile of debris and pounded on the door to the stairwell. There were sounds from below. A frightened woman with a black kerchief on her head appeared from the cellar. With terrified eyes she stared at them—covered with dirt and blood as they were, clothes hanging in shreds from the explosion. Bandi quickly explained.

"I will keep your friend's body in the cellar until you can return," the woman said. "But hurry. If the soldiers come here and find him, they will kill me, too."

They started back then, struggling together down deserted side streets, Stephen leaning heavily on Bandi's arm. Strange images floated in and out of his mind between moments of knife-searing pain.

The flowers. He saw the red flowers everywhere. Now a small child was holding a bouquet of them. But suddenly the flowers exploded, and the child shattered into pieces. Faintly, from somewhere far away, he could hear Bandi's voice saying, "Keep walking, Stephen. Please keep walking."

The White Stag. He saw it clearly for a moment, beckoning him on, but then the image faded.

Now Pali was walking toward him, twice as tall as Stephen. Stephen tried to run to him, but Pali suddenly became very small and then disappeared. He saw his father, but Apu's face was a blur; an army of AVO officers marched him away. Stephen tried to follow, to beg his father not to leave him again. His feet refused to move.

He heard music. The sound of Verdi's *Requiem* roared in his ears—or was it cannon fire?

He was falling, down, down into the dark hole again, and this time he couldn't stop.

Why were there such bright lights? Gentle hands

touched him. Somewhere a baby cried. He was being laid down on a bed, and his father's voice was saying, "Sleep, Stephen. You're home now. You're safe."

His father's voice. They hadn't taken his father away. Not yet.

He heard music again. His mother was playing Brahms's *Lullaby* on the piano. But that couldn't be. Their piano . . . where was their piano?

He slept.

When he woke it was dark and the air was chilly, but Stephen had warm blankets around him. Mária sat beside the bed, her eyes closed. He tried to talk to her, but all that came out was a moan.

She jumped. "Stephen! You're awake. Thank God."

"Am I . . . dying?" His throat felt dry. It hurt just to whisper.

"No, Stephen. The doctor—Dini's uncle—says you will live. The bullet passed close to your lung, but it did not puncture it, and he has removed it already."

"Feels . . . like he took . . . half my side."

"Don't try to talk, Stephen."

He looked around. He was in the cellar. Why was he in the cellar? It took him a minute to think this through, and then he remembered.

The fighting. The Revolution. How long ago had all that happened?

He frowned, trying to figure it out. Dini was sleeping on the cot. Grandmother, her face creased with worry, stirred diapers in a steaming kettle on the stove.

He tried again to talk. "Where's George?"

A shadow fell over Mária's face. "Bandi went to get him;

the two of them have gone for Pali."

Pali. For a few moments he'd forgotten. Stephen closed his eyes and lay very still. So they'd lived through the Revolution, had thought they'd won freedom. And now the Soviets had returned.

And Pali was dead.

The sound of footsteps on the stairs. He heard Bandi's voice and Anyu's, then soft weeping. The Szabós, Pali's parents.

Mr. Szabó walked slowly over to him and took Stephen's hand in his callused brown one. "So you are awake now. Bandi has told me how bravely you tried to rescue my boy. I thank you." Mr. Szabó stopped, took a deep breath, swallowed. "Pali tells us often of your wisdom, of the way you think things out, and of your courage under stress. My Pali . . . "

The father's voice broke. "My Pali is sometimes too quick to act, but always he tries to do what is right."

Stephen had no energy to speak or even to cry. He closed his eyes, and the murmur of voices faded into the background. He drifted in a strange world of images that appeared suddenly and were gone, a world with voices that had no bodies.

His mind cleared for a moment, and he heard George and Apu talking, their whispered voices suddenly loud in the darkness of Stephen's restless sleep.

"We must leave Hungary. Soon we will be arrested."

A pause. "But what of Stephen?"

And now there was a long silence. Stephen struggled to open his eyes, but he was unable to.

Apu, he wanted to say. Don't leave me. This time I'll go with you. But the words were thick, trapped somewhere in his head, and try as he would, they would not come out of his mouth.

He floated back out on the dark waves of sleep. When he woke later, he didn't know dream from reality.

All that remained was fear.

Chapter 18
Pali's Funeral

Tuesday, November 6

The sound of a moan.

Stephen opened his eyes.

There was a girl on the cot, just a few feet from his bed. Grandmother, her back to Stephen, swabbed a bloody gash on the girl's forehead.

The girl couldn't be much older than he was. Her dark hair stuck out wildly from her pale face, and her knuckles were white as she gripped the edge of the table. Grandmother's hands were gentle, but Stephen heard her muttered words. "So our girls fight also, and get killed alongside their brothers and fathers." Stephen groped to touch her arm. She jumped and whirled around, her full black skirt brushing his face.

"Stephen! You are awake."

He tried to talk, but his mouth felt as if it were filled with gauze. He felt her cool wrinkled hand against his lips.

"Hush! It is all right. Don't try to speak. You've been feverish for two days now." Her fingers traced the outline of a thin chain around his neck.

The medal. St. Imre, protector of Hungary's youth. His grandfather's medal rested against his chest. "You will wear it until you are well again, as Dini did." He fell back into a troubled sleep.

Apu touched his shoulder. "Stephen." His father's voice seemed stronger, more the way Stephen remembered from when he was little. "We're going to bury Pali. We cannot wait any longer."

Stephen raised himself up on his elbow. Pain knifed across his ribs, and he gasped. He swallowed, and got out the words he needed to say. "I'm coming with you."

Anyu, standing by the door, shook her head. "No, Stephen. We have nothing to give you for pain. Stay here and sleep. Pali would understand."

"I must go, Anyu." Stephen bit his lip and pulled himself into a sitting position.

His mother was silent. Apu put his arm under Stephen's elbow and helped him to his feet.

"I will see if George can get the truck," Anyu said. "There is no way you can walk."

Dini stood by him now, still weak from his own injury, holding the bedpost for support. "When we're both better, I'll cook *gulyás* for—all of us." His voice caught on the last words.

Stephen shook his head. "Not for Pali," he said. Dini looked away.

Bandi clattered down the stairs. He looked older than

twelve. He'd given his hair a determined brushing and parted it severely, instead of just brushing it back as he usually did. Stephen looked into Bandi's eyes.

It wasn't just the hair that made him seem older. Bandi had seen death, not once, but many times these past two weeks.

They were silent as George drove the truck the few blocks to Pali's home, taking side roads to avoid the Soviet tanks. Even so the sound of artillery was never far away. Pali's father stood by the door, waiting for them.

They filed in through the low doorway. Pali's mother sat beside her son's open coffin. The wrinkles on her face had been carved out by the wind and the sun during the many years she'd spent in her youth, working the land. Her tears were long spent; she said nothing as they took their place beside the wooden coffin.

Stephen's side ached; he closed his eyes for a moment against the pain. Pali's father spoke, but his words seemed to come from far away. "First the Soviets took my land. Now they have taken my only son." There was no sound in the room except for one hiccupping sob from Bandi.

Stephen opened his eyes and looked over at the coffin. Pali lay there, blood and dirt washed away.

Peaceful now. His eyes were closed. The dark smoldering anger so often reflected there, was no more.

The old man straightened his back and looked around at them all. "My wife and I will go to Csepel. The workers there have vowed to hold out to the very end. We will carry on Pali's fight for him." He picked up a folded flag from the bed and spread it over Pali's body. The jagged hole cut from the middle gaped open on Pali's chest.

George leaned over and placed a small crucifix in the casket. "Pali, this is our farewell to you. It is the last time our Scout troop will be all together. We met for one reason: to proclaim freedom. You have died for that cause. May you rest in God's peace."

Stephen looked over at Dini, leaning against the wall. Dini fumbled in his pocket and pulled out his worn green Scout neckerchief. He walked over to the coffin and laid it inside. "Pali, I pledge this for you. We'll still work for freedom, however we can."

Stephen wanted to say something, too, but the words floated around in his head. He felt dizzy. The pain in his side was worse. He sat down on the bed. George helped Pali's parents nail down the cover, then they carried the coffin outside. Stephen felt Bandi's arm under his elbow. Leaning on him, he walked the few steps outside and watched as they lowered Pali's coffin into the shallow grave in the garden. A cannon boomed somewhere close by—a hero's salute to Pali.

Pali's parents threw down the first fistfuls of dirt. George and Bandi silently covered the coffin with shovelfuls of the earth Pali had loved so much.

Then, with Bandi helping him, Stephen followed the little group back to the truck to return home.

Chapter 19
The Doctor's Plan

Thursday, November 8
to Friday, November 16

Footsteps.

Through the haze of pain he saw Anyu. "You should not have gotten up for the funeral, my Stephen." She bent over the bed, laying warm compresses against his side. "If only we had medicine to ease the spasms."

His mind drifted. He remembered having scarlet fever when he was a child. He'd wanted Anyu home with him—but she'd had to work. He pleaded with her, even cried. But she had no choice. She had to work, with Apu gone.

Grandmother sponged his burning forehead that week of the scarlet fever. She took care of all the neighborhood children whose parents worked. He could almost smell the faint odor of her lilac soap. He opened his eyes. She stood beside him, murmuring a prayer, signing a cross on his forehead with her cool fingers. He dozed off to sleep again.

The third day.

Finally the spasms were easing. He felt more alert. He looked around, wrinkling his nose against the musty smell of the cellar.

Outside, only the faint sound of faraway gunfire. A touch on his shoulder, and Apu looked down at him. His father looked stronger now. His skin had lost that transparent gray color.

"What's happening—out there?" Stephen asked.

The lines in Apu's forehead deepened. "The city's over-run—Soviet tanks and artillery everywhere. We can fight no more. Even Kilián Barracks has run out of ammunition." Apu shook his head. "Only Csepel still holds out."

Csepel. Pali's parents were there.

"It's just a matter of time. They can have only a small amount of ammunition left, even at Csepel." His father seemed able to talk now without wearing out every few words. He sat down beside Stephen on the bed. "The entire country is on strike to protest the return of the Soviets. Electricity, water, phone—these we still have—just enough to keep us alive. Everyone else refuses to work." He sighed. "It can only go on so long, Stephen. Somehow, we must get out of Hungary."

Sweat broke out on Stephen's forehead. His father was right. They had to escape. He raised himself on his elbow. "Apu. I want to get up and try to walk."

His father shook his head. "Not yet, Stephen. Perhaps tomorrow."

But it was several days before he was able to walk more than a few steps. Finally, on Friday, he felt well enough to try. He started after breakfast, pacing between the stairs and the bed, sitting for a few minutes, then trying again. Mária was bathing the baby in a tub on the table while George, exhausted, dozed in a chair.

The door above them opened, and Apu shuffled down the stairs. He set a loaf of bread on the table, then sat down wearily. "Two hours I waited for this single loaf. Hungary is dying by the day. Out on the street, hundreds of refugees are heading out of town with nothing but the clothes on their backs." He leaned back and closed his eyes. "I talked to an American journalist; he says the patrols at the border are being increased. Soon it will be impossible to get out of the country."

Fear rose in Stephen's chest.

"What will become of us?" Mária said. "Already there are rumors that the Soviets are going into the hospitals and shooting freedom fighters. George and Stephen will not escape the consequences. At the least, they will be jailed. And you, my dear Apu." She took her father's hand. "You will be arrested and taken back to prison, too. We must escape!"

Stephen rested for a minute, leaning against the table, then began pacing again. "There must be a way. Others are getting out."

"Sit down, Stephen. You're not as strong yet as you think," Apu said. "We're over one hundred miles from the border of Austria. Walking all that way is impossible with a three-week-old baby."

And with me, Stephen thought.

The door above them banged open and Dini's uncle hurried down the stairs. "I'm on my way to the hospital; I stopped to check Stephen's wound."

It was a painful ten minutes. Stephen winced as the doctor removed the dressing, then shook his head. He cleaned the wound with antiseptic and rebandaged it. "It's not infected, but it looks irritated. Are you resting as you should? You should not be pacing like a caged animal. Some walking is good for you, Stephen, but don't overdo it."

He picked up his bag, then looked around at each of them. "I see many gloomy faces in Hungary these days, and you four match them well."

Mária sighed. "We've been trying to think of some way we might escape, Uncle."

"Ah. I see many people leaving on foot, carrying their belongings in a pack on their back. But you—you have the baby, of course."

He looked at Apu. "István, you have regained your strength remarkably this past week, but a journey like this would be too much. And for you, Stephen, walking that distance is out of the question."

He rubbed his chin thoughtfully. "I have a possible solution, though it's risky. A friend of mine has been asked to drive a government truck to the border to pick up a deserted car. He's willing to take some 'helpers' with him." Stephen's heart pounded as he realized what the doctor was offering them. A government truck. The guards wouldn't stop a government truck. And there would be room for all of them. The doctor leaned forward. "My friend must go first thing in the morning. Can you be ready?"

The morning! It was too soon.

Mária gasped.

For a moment no one spoke. Then Apu stood up. "We will be ready. Thank you for this opportunity."

The doctor looked at Stephen. "It will be a difficult trip for you."

"I'll be fine. This is my first day up; I'll be stronger by tomorrow morning."

Dini's uncle smiled. "You've lost none of your determined spirit, I see. Well, if you make it out safely, you'll get the opportunity you deserve. I expect someday you will be a great musician."

The doctor's face clouded. "I wish Dini would go with you; he'd have a better chance of becoming a doctor. But he refuses. He wishes to stay here with me; and I can't deny I would miss him." He sighed. "I'll come back in the morning to see you all off." He clasped Apu's hand firmly, then turned to leave.

Anyu passed him on the stairs as she hurried down with clean clothes for the baby. He patted her arm, and she gave him a questioning look. "István will explain," he said.

Tears filled his mother's eyes as Apu told her the news. "Thank God for the miracle He has sent us. Dini's uncle is a good man." She looked anxiously at Stephen. "But tomorrow! Mother of God, how will we do this? Stephen, you're not strong enough to travel."

"I'll be fine. In the government truck we'll be able to ride all the way to the border. Besides," he teased, "with you and Grandmother beside me, I'll be well tended."

His grandmother stood in the doorway now, tears trickling silently down her cheeks. "I will not be going with you," she said. "I am too old to make such a journey. Hungary is where I was born, and it is where I will die."

She stood alone as they stared at her. "I am needed here to help with the children. What would the parents do without me if I went? You know they all work."

Apu's eyes were dark as he walked to her. He bent over, wrapping her in his arms. She stroked his thin cheek. "I am sorry, István. I cannot leave my Hungary."

Stephen leaned against the table. He knew that look on his Grandmother's face. She would not change her mind. Still, he pleaded with his eyes.

She looked away. "Come. You have little time to prepare," she said.

Anyu was at work already, scrubbing diapers in the tin washtub and hanging them up to dry by the stove. "We'll need all of these."

Her matter-of-fact voice spurred Stephen to action. Holding his side gingerly, he climbed the stairs from the cellar and went into their apartment. He pulled out all the knapsacks he could find from the old chest at the back of his closet.

He'd be wearing most of his clothes to stay warm; he bundled the few remaining things into one of the knapsacks, hesitated, and added the green Scout neckerchief from the back of his drawer.

He walked out to the parlor and looked around, trying to memorize this room that had been home to him for so long. He sat down at the piano and ran his fingers over the polished wood of the Bösendorfer. He would miss this old piano. Who knew when he would next have the opportunity to play?

If there were more time now, he would sit for a few minutes and play his Overture—his *Freedom* Overture. But Mária and the others needed his help. He climbed back down to the cellar with the rest of the knapsacks. He gave two to Mária; the baby would need the most clothes of all. She had fashioned a sling to carry the baby in front of her. "If I wear my coat so, it will just look as if I'm fat, and the guards will be fooled."

A look of fear crossed Apu's face. "Let us hope we don't have reason for the guards to see us at all."

A sudden frantic knocking on the door and Bandi burst in, Dini right behind him. "My uncle said you're leaving tomorrow. Is it true?"

Grandmother reached up to brush Dini's dark hair out of his eyes. "Yes, it is true." She put an arm around Bandi. "But I shall be staying here with both of you. Right now we must all help to get ready. Bandi, go with Mária to get the baby's things packed. Dini, you come with me. We have two chickens, a gift of the family that left yesterday. We will make a good *paprikash,* and you can begin by dicing the onions."

Stephen's side ached. He leaned against the wall to ease it. Tomorrow at this time they would be far away from the only home he had ever known. Where would they end up? He hadn't thought beyond that first step, the escape itself. He'd wanted to get out of the country, to be free, but now that the possibility was here, he felt torn in two.

He walked into the kitchen.

His grandmother stirred the chicken *paprikash* while Dini kneaded dough for *kuglóf,* Grandmother's special coffeecake. "Enough, Dini. It must sit now and raise. Go upstairs and see if Mária and George need any help."

She dipped the spoon into the pot and gave Stephen a taste of the *galuska.* Only his grandmother could make the tiny dumplings so well, but today Stephen could hardly swallow past the lump in his throat. "It's good, Grandmother, the best you've ever made." She touched his cheek gently.

Grandmother. Bringing him hot tea with honey when he was sick; holding him close when he'd fallen and skinned his knee. Lifting him up in his navy blue knitted suit—the one she'd made for him—to see himself in the mirror.

His grandmother. Her arms had rocked his cradle, tied his shoelaces, prepared his favorite *dobos* cake for his birthday meals. He remembered her helping him get ready for his first Scout outing, packing the rucksack with a flashlight, the cookware set, and his little thermos, filled with her special raspberry juice.

It was his grandmother who'd taught him first to play the piano. He remembered her beside him, her wrinkled hands gently placing his small ones on the keys.

He hugged her now, bending down to put his arms around her, resting his head for a moment on her shoulder. "I can't imagine living anywhere without you, Grandmother."

He felt her tears against his cheeks. "You are young, Stephen. You will be happy. You will finally be free. It is different for me. I am too old to start over. Hungary is my home." She touched the heavy gold medal hanging around his neck, cradling it for a moment in her palm. "You are to take this with you, my grandson."

He swallowed. When he spoke, his voice was a hoarse whisper. "But it was Grandfather's."

She nodded. "Wear it always, as he did." She tucked it inside his shirt. He felt the weight of it, warm from his Grandmother's hand.

Quickly she brushed the tears from her eyes. "Go now and call everyone. Bandi and Dini will stay, of course. We shall have a celebration meal together. Tomorrow at this time you will be on your way to freedom."

Chapter 20
A Truck Ride to Forget

Saturday, November 17

It was late that night when Stephen made his way down to the cellar. From his bed by the open coal chute, looking up through the darkness, he saw a single star. The medal rested cool and heavy against his chest.

It seemed only moments later that someone shook his sleeve. "Stephen."

It was Anyu. "You must get up now. The truck will be coming for us soon." He forced his stiff body to get up, and he followed her to the table in the dim cellar.

A pot of cocoa steamed on the back of the stove. Grandmother was cutting big slices of *kuglóf*, the coffeecake she'd made last night. She handed Stephen a piece. He took a bite, but the usually delicious cake tasted like wood shavings in his dry mouth.

He sipped the cocoa, looking down, trying not to notice her puffy eyes. She took the baby from Mária and held him on her lap. The baby shifted in his sleep. "My great-grandson." Her voice faltered. "I thank God for letting me see you."

A quick knock at the door and Bandi clattered down the stairs. "The truck's here. Dini and his uncle are outside with the driver."

Grandmother held the baby up, kissed his cheek and the warm hollow of his neck. Then she handed him back to Mária and stood up. When she spoke her voice caught. "Stephen—take the rest of the *kuglóf* with you. You have eaten hardly a thing for breakfast." He stuffed the small package into his knapsack, then followed Anyu and Apu up the stairs.

Dini's uncle stood by the truck. He put an arm around Stephen's shoulder. "I'll take care of your grandmother, Stephen. She's like our own, for the care she's given Dini since he was little. Don't worry about her."

She was coming up now. She climbed the stairs heavily, handing Stephen a folded woolen scarf. "See if you can squeeze this into one of the knapsacks. It is an extra warm one, and your journey will be cold."

The top of her head barely reached his shoulder. She looked up at him, the faint scent of lilacs mingling with the freshness of her starched apron.

Would this be the last time he smelled that fragrance, the warm odor of his grandmother?

She touched the gold medal hanging against his neck, then tucked it inside his jacket.

Kissing him, she traced the sign of the cross on his forehead. "Go with God, my beloved grandson." He wrapped his arms around her and held her one last time.

He turned away then, throwing his knapsack into the back of the truck. Bandi climbed up and stacked the suitcase and the remaining knapsacks beside them. "I'm not worried about staying. The Soviets will leave me alone because I'm too young to have fought." Bandi grinned. "Or so they think. Besides, my parents may try to get us out later—when my mother has recovered from the flu." He jumped back down from the truck.

Dini spoke, his voice hoarse. "You know, Stephen, Bandi and I won't give up the Scout troop. My uncle says he'll try to take George's place as our leader."

Stephen put an arm around each of their shoulders. Their Scout troop. He remembered a day not so long ago when Bandi had run laughing down a hill, his numbered cap sliding over one eye, glad to be allowed to join them in a game.

And Dini, his best friend from the time he was small. Always unshakable, no matter what happened. How he loved to eat! Stephen recalled him stirring *gulyás* over the campfire that last time, less than a month ago.

The three of them were silent; Stephen knew they were all remembering. Finally Dini spoke. "It almost feels as if Pali's here with us, scowling at us, and telling us to do what we must!" Stephen laughed shakily. In some ways, Pali would always be with them.

Impatient footsteps behind them. "We haven't all day, you know!" The truck driver's voice was gruff. Bandi and Dini stepped back.

The family climbed up into the old convoy truck. Stephen was the last one in. "Stay under the tarp and be quiet," the man ordered. "The Soviets should not stop us since this is a government truck, but these days, who knows?"

The baby, strapped to Mária's chest, whimpered. The driver looked startled, then angry.

"You said nothing about a baby."

Mária's face went white. "He won't betray us. If he fusses, I'll nurse him. I'll see that he's quiet."

The man jerked the canvas into place. "See that you do." He jumped into the driver's seat and started the engine.

No time to grieve. The driver took off with a lurch that threw Stephen against the side of the truck. He bit his lip as a burning pain shot across his side. Through a rip in the canvas, he caught a blurred image as the truck whipped around the corner. Dini and Bandi stood silently beside Grandmother, and Dini's uncle had his arm firmly around her.

She had never looked so small or so old.

The truck bumped and rattled its way over the roads. Stephen caught fleeting glimpses through the hole in the canvas as they wound their way around the Grand Boulevard and over St. Margaret Bridge. The Danube sparkled in the morning sun, looking as blue as it was rumored to be. No trace, except in his mind, of the river that ran red with the blood of her people.

Another ten minutes and they passed the churches of old Buda and turned onto the highway leading to Vienna. All he saw now were refugees—hundreds of men, women, and children on foot and on bicycle, many pulling little carts behind them. A small boy clung to his mother's coat, stumbling to keep up as they trudged along. The boy stared at the truck as they passed by, and Stephen saw the confusion in his eyes. The mother did not even look up.

What would happen when they came to the border? Those who weren't turned back by border patrols would have to sneak across. There were watchtowers, and guards who sent up flares, shooting at anything that moved in that sudden bright light.

And what would happen to each of them here in this truck? Stephen hunched in the corner as they bounced along, concentrating on the little patch of hillside he saw through the rip in the canvas.

After the first hour, he began to relax. The government insignia on the side of the truck seemed to be working. At each of the checkpoints, other vehicles were stopped and carefully inspected, but their truck was waved through. Then, early in the afternoon, the truck jerked to a stop. Anyu made the sign of the cross, and they waited.

He heard the voice of the Hungarian guard questioning the driver. The canvas was lifted; Stephen squinted in the light as the guard looked at them. "You must go back. I cannot let you continue on this road."

"Please," Anyu said. "No one will know if you let us through."

The guard's face was impassive. "Even if I did, you would be found out at the next checkpoint. The closer you come to the border, the heavier the security."

The driver cursed, jumped into the cab, and turned the truck around. He drove back a short distance, then turned abruptly to the right, throwing all of them against the side of the truck. "We'll take a shortcut," he shouted back. "I know a way where there will be no guards."

"Thank God," Mária whispered. She braced herself between George and the side of the truck.

The truck bounced its way over ancient dirt roads, and through meadows thick with mud. Stephen's body was one big ache; he wondered if he'd live to touch Austrian soil after all.

A sudden jolt threw him sideways. The truck shuddered to a stop. "Everybody out," the driver shouted. "We're stuck in the mud."

Stephen climbed out. The barren land was flat, with a few low-lying hills barely visible in the distance. They were on a dirt road, pockmarked with muddy potholes.

He leaned against the back of the truck and pushed, ignoring his pain. The only sounds were the muttering of the driver and Stephen's own gasping breath as the three men rocked the truck back and forth. Finally, with a sucking sound, it rolled forward.

When they climbed back in, they were covered with the thick black mud. Stephen settled wearily in the corner, huddling under his coat. The truck lurched forward. It had started to rain, an icy drizzle that blew in around the edges of the canvas. He shivered.

The baby woke up and began to fuss. "Keep him quiet!" Stephen snapped.

Mária looked startled. She pulled up her coat and began to nurse the baby; after a few minutes he settled down. The truck bounced along for what seemed a long time.

Stephen jerked upright as the truck ground to a stop. "What now?" his mother whispered. Peering through a crack in the canvas, Stephen saw the tank.

Its turret gun pointed straight at their windshield. His heart thumped.

Footsteps crunched on the frozen ground as the

commander lumbered to the back of the truck. Then a sharp, sudden brightness blinded Stephen as a soldier poked his flashlight through the opening in the canvas. "Out! All of you!" the commander ordered in Russian. Stephen didn't move quickly enough to suit him, and the officer jerked his shoulder, sending a wrenching pain through the length of his body.

He shoved his submachine gun in front of them and pointed back across the empty fields.

Anyu pleaded. "We cannot go back. We are more than one hundred miles from our home now, and we have a small baby with us."

The commander's face did not change. "Go back!" he shouted. He rammed the butt of his gun into George's back, knocking him down. Mária gave a small cry.

Stephen helped George to his feet. He looked at Apu. His father nodded, then turned and began to walk away from the guard. Stephen put his arm around Anyu and followed. Silently, they all plodded back across the empty field.

Chapter 21
Fleeing to Kapuvár

Saturday, November 17,
evening

"We'll die," Mária said. "Now we will surely die."
Stephen's side throbbed. They'd come close—so close.

It was getting colder; the baby whimpered. George pulled the extra wool scarf out of the knapsack, wrapping it over the baby's blanket. Mária's face looked pinched. George put his arm around her shoulder.

Ahead lay nothing but frozen ground. Behind them was the guard, still pointing his gun at their backs. They trudged on silently. They were out of earshot of the commander now. Apu spoke in a low voice. "If I've figured correctly, we're only a few miles east of the village of Kapuvár. I have a friend there who may be able to help us."

Anyu looked worried. "István, if you're speaking of Zoltán, we haven't seen him for years. Who knows what he's doing now, or even if he still lives in Kapuvár? He may well

143

be a Communist."

"We have no other choice, Margit. We will freeze to death if we continue walking through the night. We must trust in God, who will not desert His children."

Apu looked at him. "Stephen, when we get to that line of trees just ahead, bear to the left. If we're lucky, the commander will not notice. He'll be distracted for a few minutes while he deals with the driver of the truck."

Stephen dared not look around to see if the officer was still watching. They were almost to the trees; Stephen turned slightly, so that now each step brought them closer to the little forest of alders.

He tensed, expecting at any moment to hear the shout of the commander—or the rattle of gunshots. Every breath was painful. The cold air felt like knife-pricks in his chest.

"We're out of the guard's sight," Apu whispered. Stephen let out a long breath.

Mária slumped against a tree. He realized with a sudden shock that it had been less than three weeks since she'd given birth.

And Apu—he'd regained some strength this last week, but how long could he last, walking in this numbing cold?

"We must keep moving," Apu said. "At any moment the commander may decide to check on us." Stephen moved to Mária's side to help her. George, carrying the sleeping baby in his arms, gave him a grateful look.

The cold was bitter; the frozen earth crunched under Stephen's feet. Still, it was easier than it had been earlier, walking in the mud.

It could be no later than six or so, but the night was dark. The moon, obscured by clouds, gave just enough light to see their feet. The throbbing in his side reminded him this was not a dream. His legs seemed to be held down with great weights as he lifted first one and then the other, forcing himself to keep walking. Finally he saw lights in the distance. "Kapuvár," his father whispered. "Now we must be very careful. There is undoubtedly a curfew in effect, and if we're seen, we'll be shot." The baby whimpered, and Mária reached out to take him back.

George shook his head. "No, Mária. He's too heavy for you to carry." Stephen looked at his sister and saw the weariness on her face. She leaned on him as they moved down the darkened streets of the small town.

At last Apu held up his hand and stopped. He frowned and looked uncertainly from one to the other of two nearby houses, both with wide, sagging porches. Finally he turned into the yard of the closer one. "I pray this is the right house," he murmured.

Anyu's face was strained. "If it is not, we may not get a second chance." Apu took her hand as they moved silently toward the back of the house into the sheltering shadows of the building. Stephen and the others followed.

Apu knocked on the door of the house, while the rest of them waited a few steps back in the darkness. Stephen's heart hammered against his ribs. If it was the wrong house, who knew what might happen? They could well be reported to the AVO.

And even if this was Zoltán's house, there was no guarantee that he'd help them.

Finally the door opened. A stocky man squinted out into the darkness, stared at Apu, frowned in puzzlement. Apu leaned forward. "Zoltán! Do you remember me? István Kôváry?"

At last a smile spread across the man's face. "István. I haven't seen you for years." He looked at the rest of them standing silently in the shadows.

"Ah. I see what you are up to. Well, come in, all of you. You frightened me with your late-night knock."

Now they were in the house, and Zoltán was heating great tubs of hot water for them to wash off the mud that covered them. Anyu handed Stephen a steaming bucket. The warmth felt good as he sponged his aching body. "We must clean your wound, my son." He winced as she helped him remove the bandage. It was more tender than it had been for several days now.

"Damn!" Stephen pulled away as Anyu pressed the steaming cloth against the red rawness of his wound. Immediately he felt ashamed, using such language in front of his mother.

"It's all right, Stephen," she said. "I know how it must hurt. It looks red, and a little swollen. I pray it isn't infected."

Zoltán's wife, sleepy-eyed but cheerful, hurried into the room and began to prepare a meal for them. Stephen relaxed; his pain eased. He sat with the others at the round table in the simple kitchen, drinking hot tea with honey and eating big bites of homemade bread with smoked *paprikash* sausage. Apu and Zoltán talked and talked, catching up on these last several years of their lives.

When the meal was over, Apu pushed back his chair. "Zoltán, my friend, I've imposed on your hospitality after all these years. Now I must ask an even greater favor. Do you know someone who could lead us across the border?" Zoltán frowned. He sat silently, his head down. Apu sighed.

He pulled a worn map from his jacket pocket. "Or perhaps you could mark a safe route on this map, and we can continue on our own under cover of darkness."

Zoltán's voice was grave. "We're about eight miles from the border, but you must cross a swamp. It would be foolhardy for you to go without a guide. I'll do my best to get one for you, but I can't promise anything. There are only a few men who know how to navigate these treacherous waterways. Many have died trying to do it on their own."

He stood up and pulled on a heavy leather jacket. "Anna, make them comfortable. I'll be back as soon as I can." He hurried out the door, jumped on an old bicycle parked by the side of the house, and wheeled silently away into the darkness.

Anna bustled into the other room. "I will open up some cots. Then you may sleep for a while. Zoltán will probably not be back for at least two hours." Within minutes, she had them comfortably settled.

Stephen lay awake, staring into the darkness. He could hear Mária's quiet breathing as she dozed on the couch, and sucking noises as the baby nursed. What if someone had seen Zoltán leaving and reported them to the police?

What if the so-called guide betrayed them? Or the baby cried as they tried to get by the border guards? He reached up and felt the heavy medal around his neck. His grandfather had worn this throughout his life. Now it was his—a pledge of his grandmother's belief in him.

Pali had believed in him, too.

We will live, Stephen thought. My father has returned, and we will live. We'll get our chance to live in freedom.

But his fear remained, and he shifted restlessly on his cot, waiting.

Chapter 22
Led by the White Stag

Sunday, November 18

A gentle creaking. The front door opened. Stephen was awake instantly, shivering in the cold draft. He sat up. His father was on his feet already; the rest of them waited in silence.

Zoltán's stocky shadow filled the doorway. "A man I trust will be here soon; he will carry you in his wagon to the swamp. Then a friend of his will take you through the marsh by boat. He is a man who knows it well; he grew up beside it."

Zoltán hesitated. "There's one difficulty. The guide insists on payment to take you across the canal and the swamp—two thousand forints."

Silence in the room.

Apu's shoulders slumped. "I have five hundred forints, and no more." He took the crumpled bills from his pocket and put them on the table.

George searched his own pockets and put that money on the table also. Anyu counted it. "Seven hundred-fifty forints," she said. "What are we to do?" Her voice shook, and Apu put his arm around her.

Zoltán rubbed his chin. "We have only 250 forints in the house, but I gladly give it to you. Have you any jewelry? He would take that as payment."

Mária took off her watch. "My darling George, your birthday present to me."

George silently added his own watch to the pile on the table. "We still have not enough," Apu said. "If only I, too, had a watch."

There was a long silence. George paced to the end of the room and stared out the window into the black night. The baby whimpered, then settled back into sleep. Stephen reached inside his shirt and took off the medal of St. Imre. It rested heavy and warm in his hand, the gold gleaming as it caught a ray of moonlight from the window. He raised it to his lips and kissed it. "You would understand, Grandmother." He walked over and laid it with the little pile on the table.

Apu put his hand on Stephen's shoulder. "Your grandfather would be proud. He prized freedom above all else." He looked at Zoltán. "We have enough. The medal will make up the two thousand forints."

Outside, the crunch of wheels on frozen ground. Zoltán stood up. "The wagon's here. Hurry. Only a few hours until dawn, and you must be across the border before then."

George picked up the suitcase, but Zoltán shook his head. "No room for that in the boat. Put what you can in your knapsacks; the rest I'll keep here for you."

A quiet whinny under the window. They filed outside. Zoltán gave Apu a bear hug. "God go with you, István." He took Stephen's hand in his. "István's son, take courage. May we meet again some day, in freedom."

Stephen climbed after the others into the back of the wagon, protecting his side cautiously. The farmer cracked his whip; the buggy rolled along between the barren fields. Once more Stephen braced himself, biting his lip when they hit sudden bumps. They came to the crest of a small hill.

The farmer pointed. "There—see those lights? That is Austria."

Stephen stared at the twinkling points of brightness on the horizon, then turned to look at the barren hills of Hungary behind him. In front of him lay his future; behind him his past.

Between the two lay the swamp.

He could see the hazy outline of the bulrush with two lonely trees silhouetted against the sky. A chilly breeze carried the odor of the marsh to his nostrils. He wrinkled his nose, smelling the stagnant water and decaying weeds.

The farmer stopped the wagon. "You must walk now. The wagon wheels will sink if I go any farther; the ground isn't frozen this close to the swamp." Silently Stephen fell into line behind the farmer. The distance that had looked so short stretched into the darkness. They climbed one small hill after another, and still the farmer strode on, his boots making sucking noises in the mud. George carried the baby. Mária, exhausted, struggled to keep up.

She stumbled, then stifled a cry as she slipped in the mud and fell. Stephen pulled her up, feeling her limp heaviness.

"Stephen, I'm frightened. I have no strength left. I don't

know if I can make it."

"Lean against me. We'll be at the boat soon." Finally he saw its faint outline, low and square, nearly invisible in the darkness of the bulrushes. The farmer waved a silent good-bye.

The waiting fisherman stamped his cold feet impatiently and signaled them over to the boat. "You have the payment?" Apu pressed the money and jewelry into the man's hand. He glanced at the watches, then studied the medal for a moment, holding it up to the moonlight.

He grunted. "It's well made. It will bring many forints." He shoved the money and jewelry into his jacket pocket and climbed into the boat, situating himself at a plank at the back. "Get in now, all of you. Hurry." Stephen held out his hand to Mária and helped her into the flatbottomed boat. She slumped on the bottom.

The rest of them clambered in. The boat sank lower and lower in the water. Stephen was last; he climbed cautiously into the front of the boat.

There were no seats except for the plank in the back where the fisherman sat. He pushed off with one oar. The boat glided silently into the swamp. Stephen strained his eyes against the darkness; he could see nothing. The only sounds were the steady slap of the oars as they hit the water and the scratchy whisper of bulrush against the side of the boat.

They could never find their way out of this swamp alone.

"Stay as low as possible," the man whispered. "If there's a flare, freeze. Only what moves can be seen clearly."

The boat slowed as they moved through a tangle of weeds; the fisherman, muttering an oath, used the oar to push them clear.

They pulled into one of the side canals of the maze that was the road system within the swamp. The moon was hidden now, behind a cloud. There were no landmarks; only bulrush, black as the night they moved through. Stephen looked up, grateful for the stars that flickered in the sky above, giving some kind of light to this dark dream.

Suddenly there was a cry; it sounded like a child. It came from one of the side canals off to the right. Their guide cursed under his breath and turned the boat in the direction of the sound. Within moments Stephen saw the shadows of a man and woman in the bog ahead of them.

The man held a small child over his head; the child sobbed as the man sank deeper into the thick mud. Already it was up to his waist. "Help! Help us, please!" the woman cried out.

The guide glared at her. "Shhh! There's nothing we can do. There's no room to put three more people in this boat. We'd all sink."

Anyu reached out and touched the guide's sleeve. "They will drown. We must try. We'll all move further back in the boat."

"You're crazy. If this boat sinks, I'll leave you here and find my own way back to safety."

Anyu's voice was calm. "We will not sink. God will be with us."

The fisherman swore and rowed toward the woman.

"My baby! Please save my baby." The woman splashed the muddy water, struggling to reach them, but each movement pushed her further down into the bog.

"Hold still or you'll sink deeper," the fisherman growled.

"You! Boy in the front of the boat!" He pointed his oar at

Stephen. "If anyone pulls them in, it will have to be you. We cannot try to change positions now." He edged the boat closer.

Stephen knelt stiffly, his aching knees pressed against the rough wood. He eased the little girl from her father's grasp and into the boat. Anyu opened her coat to put the shivering child inside. "Mama! I want my mama," the little girl whimpered.

"Shhh. There now. She'll be here with you soon," Anyu said.

Stephen leaned back out of the boat and grasped the woman's arms. Her body was an unyielding weight, caught in the thick muck.

He pulled. The mud loosened its hold and her weight moved suddenly toward him.

He braced himself. The boat rocked violently. The fisherman was right. They were crazy to try this. He eased the woman into the boat, his arms aching with the effort. The woman slumped to the bottom and huddled there, shivering. Stephen hesitated, then took off his coat and handed it to her. The chilly breeze pricked through his sweater with icy needles. The murky waters of the marsh lapped just inches from the top rim of the boat.

Maybe the fisherman could take them to safety, then return for the man.

No. He dare not suggest that. The mud was halfway up the man's chest already. If they left, the man would drown.

The fisherman pulled a board from the side of the boat and flung it onto the thick mud. "Hurry. We've no time to waste. Push yourself up on this." The man twisted, struggling to work his feet loose from the swamp bottom.

Stephen leaned out of the boat, stretching as far as he dared, the edge of the boat pressing painfully against his sore side. He grasped the man's sodden coat collar. He could hear his mother's voice murmuring behind him as she prayed. Frigid water sloshed around his knees; his legs were numb.

The man grunted as he turned from side to side, pushing his weight against the board. A sucking sound, and his feet pulled suddenly loose. He fell across the bow of the boat. It lurched, and icy water poured into the side. The man scrambled in.

"We're sinking," Mária whispered.

"Now you've done it!" The fisherman poled to a reedy area at the edge of the swamp. "Your only chance is by foot now. You'll probably all drown."

The boat rocked between the reeds until it came to rest. "Get out," the guide ordered. He pointed at Stephen. "You first. Feel for solid ground before you step, or you'll sink."

Stephen stepped quickly into the reeds at the edge. His foot went down; cold mud oozed into the top of his boot.

Heart pounding, he felt with his other foot and found a strip of firmer ground. Pulling his mud-soaked boot loose, he edged forward and reached out to help Mária. Her hand trembled as she clambered out. Her weight sank against him; she seemed hardly able to stand.

The others scrambled out, one by one. The guide poled the boat a little forward, climbed out, and shoved it into the bushes. "I'm a fool for not leaving you. We'll sink in this bog."

He tied the boat, then moved to the front of the line. "You've only a few inches of solid ground. Go single file, and follow me exactly."

They edged their way along the path between the reeds. George first, behind the guard, carrying the baby. The little one stretched in his sleep and let out a small cry. "For God's sake, keep that baby quiet." The guide glared at George. "Border guards patrol this area in boats. If you're captured, you won't get another chance."

Anyu's face went white. She looked at Apu, then bent to help the little girl they'd just rescued, who was whimpering quietly. The child's parents seemed in shock as they stumbled along with their heads down.

Mária was next. Stephen tried to keep a hand under her elbow to steady her, but the narrowness of the path made it impossible.

In just moments, she stumbled. She stepped clumsily to the side to catch her balance, and sank into the mud. Struggling to keep his own footing, Stephen clutched her under the arms and tugged. Her legs pulled loose from the oozing ground with a loud sucking sound.

A flare went up.

One glimpse of Mária's mud-splattered face, terrified in that bright light. Then everything went dark again. He heard only the racing of his own heart. Had the guards seen them? He stood still, listening for the sound of a motor.

The night was quiet. A mist rose over the marsh. Mária sank to the ground. "I can't," she murmured.

George handed the baby to Anyu and worked his way back to them. He stood next to Mária, teetering for balance between the reeds. "Mária, it's only a little farther. We'll help you."

She shook her head. "No, George. My legs . . . no strength."

A shuddering roar filled the air. The guide cursed. He picked up the little girl. "Move!" he growled, and gave Apu a sharp nudge forward.

Behind him Anyu moaned. "No . . . my Mária." The guide ignored her pleas; he pushed Anyu and Apu ahead of him along the muddy path.

Stephen looked at George and then down at Mária. "Could we carry her?"

George shook his head. "The path's too narrow. And the weight . . . we would sink in this mud." Mária muttered to herself, half words, half broken sobs.

Stephen crouched beside her. "Mária, try. It's just a bit farther." She shook her head. She looked up, her face suddenly startled. She stared behind Stephen at some spot over his shoulder.

"The White Stag!" she whispered.

Stephen looked over his shoulder. Nothing. Only the dark night and the mist rising over the marsh. Was she hallucinating as he had done that night at Kilián Barracks?

Mária rose to her knees. She held tightly to Stephen's wrist with one hand and to George with her other. "There. Just as Apu told us—in the mist." A sudden idea hit Stephen. He looked at George, who nodded slightly.

"Mária," Stephen said gently. "Where's the White Stag?"

She looked confused for a moment, then pointed over Stephen's shoulder. "There. Up ahead. Where Apu went."

"Show us," George said. "Come, we'll help you."

Mária hesitated. "So tired . . . " she murmured.

"We'll follow the White Stag," Stephen said. "Like Magyar and his brother."

George held her face in his hands. "To freedom, Mária."

She shuddered a sigh and held up her hands. They lifted her to her feet. The sound of the motor was louder now. The border patrol was close, in one of the side canals not far from them. There was no place for them to hide, no trees, no bushes. Only the bulrush, dark and stinking, along the water's edge.

Stephen strained his eyes to see the shadow of the fisherman ahead of them on the misty trail. Would there be more guards at the end of this trail?

His heart jumped.

Faintly visible a few dozen yards past the guide, a tiny bit of red and white cloth fluttered at the top of a stick. A border marker!

"There!" Mária said hoarsely. "The White Stag. Can't you see it?"

Another flare. They froze.

His hands and feet were numb. Blinded by the flare, he could see nothing.

He edged forward again, feeling his way. The sky was getting lighter; it was almost dawn.

Their time was nearly up. How could a few dozen yards take so long to travel?

Mária stumbled. Stephen grasped her hand, fought to hold her up. George's breath rasped as he struggled to support her from the other side. She regained her balance.

"That's it, Mária," Stephen whispered. Slowly, slowly, they inched forward. She kept her eyes focused on the White Stag in front of them as she stumbled along the path.

They walked a tightrope across the narrow strip of solid ground, on either side of them, the treacherous mud.

A thin wailing cry from the trail ahead of him.

The baby.

Stephen's heart seemed to stop. Were there border guards near?

Hurry. They had to hurry.

But the path was so narrow.

He saw the marker clearly now. A slender cane of wood no higher than his shoulder, the fluttering pennant just a few inches square—the Austrian flag. Close. They were so close.

He dragged Mária now, trying to hold her weight up, George lifting her from behind. No sound but the gasping of their breath and the whisper of marsh grass against their legs.

Then finally, finally, something firm under his feet.

Solid ground. They were out of the swamp. Just a few steps more.

His breath shuddering in his chest, he reached out and touched the marker. He wrapped his numb fingers around that slender shaft of wood with the small red-and-white flag atop it.

Austria.

They had made it.

Mária collapsed into George's arms and wept. He eased her gently to the ground and sat there, holding her. The others gathered around them, holding them, crying with them.

"Mother of God, thank you," Anyu said. "We have journeyed from death into life." She placed the baby in Mária's outstretched arms.

Mária laid her cheek against her baby's face. "You are safe now, little one," she whispered. "Finally, we are free."

She stared back into the mist. "The White Stag led us," she said to Stephen wonderingly.

"Yes," Stephen said. "The White Stag led us."

"You are all fools," the guide said. "But I am glad you are here now, safe on Austrian soil." He grasped Apu's hand with both of his. "I must go back before the border patrol finds my boat."

Brushing past Stephen, he pressed something cold and heavy into his hand. "The rest I will keep, but this goes with you. God be with you." The guide disappeared into the bulrush.

Stephen looked down. Grandfather's medal. Saint Imre, protector of Hungary's youth.

Anyu wept as she fastened it around his neck. "For freedom," she said. "Our greatest gift, Stephen. May we never forget."

Epilogue

Two hundred thousand Hungarian people, like the Kôvárys, escaped to Austria in the months following the 1956 Revolution. From there, many of them emigrated to the United States and Canada, where they found jobs and made new lives for themselves. Helen M. Szablya, coauthor of this book, was one of those who escaped. Much of Stephen's story is based on the real-life experiences the Szablya family had during and after the Revolution.

Like Stephen's sister Mária, Helen was a student at the Technological University at the time of the Revolution, and her husband John, like George in the story, taught at the University. The night the Revolution started the Szablyas were at the Parliament Building while the crowds shouted for Imre Nagy. Like Mária, Helen was pregnant and delivered her baby during the Revolution (though Helen, unlike Mária, was able to make it to the hospital!).

The Szablyas, like Stephen's family, escaped across the Austrian border after their Revolution failed. They had with them their baby and two other young children.

Though the Szablyas' escape was different from Stephen's, they were captured three times before they crossed over to Austria. It was not as dramatic as sinking in the swamp, but it was a frightening experience and one that Helen Szablya and her family will always remember.

In many ways the Revolution in Hungary serves as a model for what happens in any country when people revolt against tyranny. We see similar patterns emerge in Czechoslovakia in 1969, in Poland in the 1980's—even in the China uprising that culminated in the massacre at Tiananmen Square.

The writers and students in the country almost always are in the forefront, expressing the pain, leading the demonstrations. The government eventually reacts to squash the revolt, often violently, with tanks used against its own people.

In Hungary, the years following the Revolution were painful ones. Thousands of freedom fighters were arrested, and executed or deported. Even the young teenagers like Stephen who fought were not exempt; many of them were held in prisons until they were eighteen and could be legally prosecuted. Hundreds of these young people were executed at age eighteen for the "crime" of defending their country's freedom.

But in some ways, the Hungarian Revolution eventually succeeded. Never again could Soviet Russia pose before the world as the benefactor of mankind. "The Hungarian dead have torn that mask off. Their fingers hold its tatters in their graves," said writer Archibald MacLeish after the Revolution.

The Kádár government realized eventually it could never again impose the same power over the Hungarian people. By the end of the sixties the government began to introduce economic reforms, and by 1985 Hungary was in better economic condition than any of the other Central and Eastern European countries.

Then, once more, Hungary was destined to play a major part in the spread of world freedom. In 1989, Hungary's part in helping East German refugees escape to Austria triggered a wave of events that led to the collapse of the Soviet Union and the tearing down of the Berlin Wall. Freedom swept across Central and Eastern Europe. In early 1990 free elections were held in Hungary for the first time since 1946.

Hungary is now free. October 23, the first day of the 1956 revolution, is celebrated as a national holiday.

And today, once again, Scouting is legal in Hungary.

GLOSSARY

Anyu—(ON-you) Hungarian word for mother (Stephen and Mária's mother, in this case)

Apu—(AW-poo) Hungarian word for Father (Stephen and Mária's)

AVO—(AWV-oh) Security Police in Hungary, hated by the people for their methods of arresting and torturing innocent citizens

Bandi—(BAWN-dee) Stephen's friend, youngest boy in Scout troop

Bem—(Bem) Famous Polish general who helped the Hungarians fight in the 1848-1849 War of Independence.

bukta—(BOOK-taw) plum-filled pastry

Cardinal Mindszenty—(MEND-sen-tee) leader of the Roman Catholic Church in Hungary. Imprisoned by both the Nazis and the Communists. Most of the Hungarians considered him the symbol of free Hungary.

Dini—(DI-nee) Stephen's best friend

dobos cake—(DOH-bohsh) torte, consisting of many thin, alternating layers of sponge cake and chocolate cream, topped with burnt caramel

galuska—(GAW-loosh-kaw) little dumplings; a favorite Hungarian dish

George—(George) Mária's husband; also leader of the Scout troop.

Gerô—(GEH-ruh) The Communist Party Secretary and Prime Minister at the time of the outbreak of the Revolution; ordered to shoot the freedom fighters

gulyás—(GOO-yash) A favorite Hungarian meal; a stew of meat, paprika, potatoes, and onions. ("Gulyás" literally means cowboy; gulyás soup is the stew cowboys make in the fields.)

Imre Nagy—(EEM-reh Nawdg) Became Prime Minister (head of the cabinet) during the Revolution. A Communist, but much beloved by the Hungarian people. Believed in the changes the people wanted, and tried to make those come about. He was ultimately executed after the crushing of the Revolution.

István—(EESHT-vawn) Stephen's father; the name is the Hungarian form of the name "Stephen"

Jóska Káldor—(YOSH-kaw KAL-door) Stephen's classmate, whose father was a member of the hated AVO

Kapuvár—(KAW-poo-vawr) A small town in Hungary near the Austrian border

Kossuth, Lajos—(KOH-shoot LO-yosh) Beloved charismatic leader of the 1848-1849 War of Independence in Hungary

Kossuth nóta—(KOH-shoot NOHT-aw) Kossuth's (war) song

kulacs—(KOOL-awch) a small canteen, covered with horse skin, used by cowboys and shepherds to carry their drink for the day

kuglóf—(KOOG-loaf) a kind of coffeecake

lángos—(LAN-ghosh) deep fried bread dough, a favorite delicacy in Hungary

Lenin—(Lenin) Founder of the Union of Soviet Socialist Republics, considered the father of Communist Russia

Liszt—(List) Famous Hungarian composer who lived in the 1800's, considered by some to be the world's greatest pianist

Magyar—(MAGD-yar) The Hungarian word for "Hungarian." According to legend, Prince Magyar and his brother Prince Hunor led their people, the Hungarians (Magyars) and the Huns, respectively, to the present Hungary.

Maléter, Pál—(MAWL-ay-tare Pahl) Hungarian Colonel who led the freedom fighters at Kilián Barracks and later became Minister of Defense. He was ultimately executed after the crushing of the Revolution.

Mária—(MAWR-ee-ah) Stephen's older sister

Margit—(MAWR-geet) Stephen's mother's name

Minister—(minister) Member of the Cabinet

Molotov cocktails—(MAWL-aw-tawf cocktails) Home-made gasoline bombs

Mr. Tóth, Antal—(Toth AWN-tawl) Stephen's teacher: a Communist who became disillusioned and joined the Hungarian freedom fighters

Pali—(PAWL-ee) Stephen's friend and rival

paprikash—(POP-ree-kawsh) proper Hungarian spelling is "paprikás," but this meal is known in the USA as "paprikash." A dish prepared with a lot of paprika spice thrown onto sauteed onions. Then any kind of meat, or even plain potatoes are added. This is then cooked in water, until meat is tender. Depending on the meat the dish is called: chicken, veal, potato, etc. paprikás.

Petôfi—(PET-oh-fee) Famous poet whose words inspired freedom fighters in both the 1848 and 1956 wars of independence

Radio Building—Center of all government communications in Budapest in 1956. On the evening of October 23, the people assembled there to try to get the Sixteen Points broadcast to the people. At this site, the first shots of the Revolution were fired.

tök—(tuhk) vegetable, similar to zucchini; in the United Kingdom it is called "vegetable marrow"

vidra—(VEE-draw) An otter

ABOUT THE AUTHORS

HELEN SZABLYA

It is nearly impossible to separate the life of Helen Szablya from her work. Dedicated to promoting freedom from institutions that repress, this award-winning journalist has written and lectured passionately on the subject of the Hungarian Revolution of 1956. *The Fall of the Red Star*, told through fourteen-year-old Stephen Kovary and his family, is based on the true-life accounts of her own family's dramatic struggle for freedom. Helen's experience is paralleled by Stephen's sister Maria, who was a university student and delivered her baby at the time of the Revolution.

Born in Budapest, Hungary, Helen Szablya escaped to Canada and later settled in the state of Washington. She earned a bachelor of arts degree in foreign languages and literature from Washington State University. Fluent in six languages, she worked as a translator and interpreter for many years. Her dream of becoming a writer was postponed until 1965, when the last member of her immediate family escaped from Hungary.

Currently an Honorary Consul of the Republic of Hungary, Helen Szablya has been awarded the Jozsef Antall Memorial Medal for Outstanding Service to Hungary, the Medal of the 1956 Revolution by the Guardian of Liberty (Munich, Germany), and the Freedom Foundation's George Washington Honor Medal.

PEGGY KING ANDERSON

Enlisted by Ms. Szablya as an established, award-winning children's book writer, Ms. Anderson helped write *The Fall of the Red Star* from a child's point of view. She began to rewrite the story in 1986, spending much time researching Hungary and the Revolution of 1956. By the time Ms. Anderson had finished the final rewrite, Helen Szablya proclaimed her an honorary Hungarian.

Peggy King Anderson's previous books include *Safe at Home!*, *First Day Blues*, and *Coming Home*. She has won several awards, including the 1988 Magazine Merit Award for Fiction from the Society of Children's Book Writers and Illustrators.